The Catsgiving Feast
by WITHDRAWN

Kathi Daley

D1707423

This book is a work of fiction. Names, characters, places, and incidents either are products of the author's imagination or are used fictitiously. Any resemblance to actual events or locales or persons, living or dead, is entirely coincidental.

Copyright © 2018 by Katherine Daley

Version 1.0

I want to thank the very talented Jessica Fischer for the cover art.

I so appreciate Bruce Curran, who is always ready and willing to answer my cyber questions; Jayme Maness for helping out with the book clubs; and Peggy Hyndman for helping sleuth out those pesky typos.

And, of course, thanks to the readers and bloggers in my life, who make doing what I do possible.

And a special thank you to Nancy Farris, Patty Liu, Sharon Guagliardo, and Pam Curran for submitting recipes.

Thank you to Randy Ladenheim-Gil for the editing.

And finally, I want to thank my husband Ken for allowing me time to write by taking care of everything else.

Books by Kathi Daley
Come for the murder, stay for the romance.

Zoe Donovan Cozy Mystery:
Halloween Hijinks
The Trouble With Turkeys
Christmas Crazy
Cupid's Curse
Big Bunny Bump-off
Beach Blanket Barbie
Maui Madness
Derby Divas
Haunted Hamlet
Turkeys, Tuxes, and Tabbies
Christmas Cozy
Alaskan Alliance
Matrimony Meltdown
Soul Surrender
Heavenly Honeymoon
Hopscotch Homicide
Ghostly Graveyard
Santa Sleuth
Shamrock Shenanigans
Kitten Kaboodle
Costume Catastrophe
Candy Cane Caper
Holiday Hangover
Easter Escapade
Camp Carter
Trick or Treason
Reindeer Roundup
Hippity Hoppity Homicide
Firework Fiasco

Henderson House
Holiday Hostage – *December 2017*

Zimmerman Academy The New Normal
Zimmerman Academy New Beginnings
Ashton Falls Cozy Cookbook

Tj Jensen Paradise Lake Mysteries by Henery Press:

Pumpkins in Paradise
Snowmen in Paradise
Bikinis in Paradise
Christmas in Paradise
Puppies in Paradise
Halloween in Paradise
Treasure in Paradise
Fireworks in Paradise
Beaches in Paradise
Thanksgiving in Paradise – *Fall 2019*

Whales and Tails Cozy Mystery:

Romeow and Juliet
The Mad Catter
Grimm's Furry Tail
Much Ado About Felines
Legend of Tabby Hollow
Cat of Christmas Past
A Tale of Two Tabbies
The Great Catsby
Count Catula
The Cat of Christmas Present
A Winter's Tail
The Taming of the Tabby

Frankencat
The Cat of Christmas Future
Farewell to Felines
A Whisker in Time
The Catsgiving Feast

Writers' Retreat Southern Seashore Mystery:

First Case
Second Look
Third Strike
Fourth Victim
Fifth Night
Sixth Cabin
Seventh Chapter

Rescue Alaska Paranormal Mystery:

Finding Justice
Finding Answers
Finding Courage
Finding Christmas – *December 2018*

A Tess and Tilly Mystery:

The Christmas Letter
The Valentine Mystery
The Mother's Day Mishap
The Halloween House
The Thanksgiving Trip

The Inn at Holiday Bay:

Haunting by the Sea:
Homecoming by the Sea
Secrets by the Sea
Missing by the Sea
Christmas by the Sea – *December 2018*

Sand and Sea Hawaiian Mystery:
Murder at Dolphin Bay
Murder at Sunrise Beach
Murder at the Witching Hour
Murder at Christmas
Murder at Turtle Cove
Murder at Water's Edge
Murder at Midnight

Seacliff High Mystery:
The Secret
The Curse
The Relic
The Conspiracy
The Grudge
The Shadow
The Haunting

Road to Christmas Romance:
Road to Christmas Past

Chapter 1

Tuesday, November 13

My name is Caitlin Hart and I am marrying the love of my life, Cody West, in exactly four days, three hours, and eleven minutes. While there appear to be a few challenges on the horizon, I am determined that nothing is going to ruin my special day. Not the major storm that's supposed to blow in by tomorrow evening, not Cody's obnoxious cousin who showed up with Cody's mother despite Cody's intentionally not inviting him, not the black eye I now sport after falling into the bedroom door after tripping over my dog Max, and not the new wedding venue I must find after St. Patrick's, the church I have attended my entire life and the church I've dreamed of getting married in since I was old enough to dream of getting married, has closed for repairs following a small fire that appears to have been caused by an electrical malfunction.

"We might have a problem," my sister, Siobhan Finnegan, said to me after she'd tentatively entered my small seaside cabin through the side door.

"Of course we do," I answered, rolling my eyes. "Did the florist come down with the plague or did the bakery burn to the ground?"

"Worse."

"What can be worse than a bakery burning to the ground?"

"The bakery owner, Sally Enderling, was found dead this morning by her assistant."

I placed my hand on my heart. "Oh no. I'm so sorry. What happened?"

"I spoke to Finn," Siobhan referred to her husband, Deputy Ryan Finnegan. "It looks like someone came up behind her and hit her with an object they believe, based on the size and shape of the wound, was a rolling pin. She was found facedown in the walk-in refrigerator."

"That's awful. The poor woman. I can't imagine who would do such a thing." I didn't know Sally well, although we did run into each other from time to time, and she seemed nice enough. She'd moved to the island four years ago from Seattle, but once she settled in, she jumped right into public service by running for a board position with the local chamber of commerce. She'd done a bang-up job, from what I understood, and there was even talk of her running for a seat on the town council in an upcoming election. I knew she was married to an accountant who had an office in Seattle but had arranged to work remotely a good deal of the time. I couldn't imagine who would want to harm the woman. "Are there any suspects?"

"One," Siobhan said. I couldn't help but notice that she seemed to be cringing as she spoke. "It seems, based on what we know at this moment, the last person to see Sally alive was Cody's mother."

I closed my eyes, took a deep breath, and blew it out slowly. "Cody's mother?"

Siobhan nodded. "That's what Finn said. According to Sally's assistant, Carla, Cody's mother went to see Sally yesterday afternoon shortly before closing."

"Why would Mrs. West go to see Sally?"

"It seems she wasn't a fan of the plain white cake you chose, so she decided to speak to Sally about adding a different filling to each layer. Sally very nicely informed her that you'd specifically requested a simple frosting, and that you'd stated quite clearly that you didn't want filling of any flavor, at which point Cody's mother started yelling at her."

I slowly counted to ten before continuing in a much sterner voice than I'd intended. "Why on earth would Mrs. West yell at Sally?"

Siobhan crossed her arms over her chest. "Hey, don't shoot the messenger."

I closed my eyes and blew out a breath. "I'm sorry. It's not your fault. I didn't mean to shout. Go on."

"Carla had to pick up her daughter from dance class, so she left in the middle of the conversation, but based on what Carla told Finn, Cody's mother was very forcefully pointing out that she would be the one paying for the cake, which made *her* the customer, which in her mind required Sally to make the changes she was requesting."

I tossed back my head and threw up my arms. "That woman insisted on paying for the cake. I never asked her to contribute a dime to this wedding, but she showed up a week before she was scheduled to arrive with Cody's totally irritating cousin in tow and started making demands. Paying for the cake was one of those demands."

Siobhan took my hand in hers. "I know, sweetie. And you've done such a good job of sucking it up and allowing her to participate. I don't think the cake or the filling or the fact that Cody's mom seems to be torturing you for not having the wedding in Florida is the point of this conversation, however. The point is that Mrs. West threatened to hurt Sally, and now she's dead."

"She threatened to hurt her?" I screeched.

Siobhan nodded. "Two women who were passing by the bakery told Finn that Mrs. West insisted Sally make the changes she wanted or suffer the consequences. I suppose she could have meant many things by that, but the sheriff is taking her threat seriously. Finn said he's on his way to the island to question her himself. Finn's been instructed to bring her in."

I fell back into a chair, which, fortunately, was directly behind me. That was it. God was definitely sending me a sign that I wasn't supposed to marry Cody. There really was no other explanation. "So Sally died yesterday afternoon?"

"Finn thinks so. He's waiting for the medical examiner to say exactly when she died, but Carla said Sally had on the same clothes she'd worn yesterday, and it didn't appear she ever went home."

"Wouldn't her husband know that for certain?"

"He was in Virginia visiting his mother, who's been ill. No one realized Sally hadn't gone home until Carla showed up for work this morning."

I took several deep breaths as I tried to steady my suddenly very shaky nerves. "Does Cody know?"

"Finn was going to track him down and talk to him right after he hung up with me."

This wasn't going to go over well at all. "He went to the north shore this afternoon to take some photos for the story on the fire at the old community church. I doubt he's back yet. Still, he should be available by cell." I stood up and took yet another breath to strengthen my resolve. "I suppose I should head over to Finn's office."

"Finn said no. He was going to explain things to Mrs. West when he picked her up. He'll call after she speaks to the sheriff, but he didn't want you anywhere near the office when he speaks to her. I think all we can do is wait."

Well, that was just fantastic. There was nothing I liked better than waiting on the sidelines while the world crumbled around me.

"Cait? Are you okay?" Siobhan asked when I didn't answer.

I nodded. "I'm fine. I trust Finn. I'm sure he has everything under control." I glanced at my dog. "I think I'm going to take Max for a run."

******

Later that afternoon, I decided waiting was for the birds and headed to the newspaper to see how Cody was doing. Finn didn't want me anywhere near his office while the sheriff was on the island, but the newspaper was all the way next door, so I was sure it would be fine.

It wasn't.

After being scolded by Finn about following directions and actions having consequences and a whole bunch of other malarkey, I decided to go down the street to Coffee Cat Books, where I knew I would find people who loved me *and* wouldn't yell at me.

"Cait, what are you doing here?" My best friend and maid of honor Tara O'Brian asked. "I thought you were taking the day off to work on wedding stuff."

"I was, but then the woman making my wedding cake was murdered and Cody's mother is the prime suspect, so I decided angsting over a new venue could wait."

Tara's mouth fell open. "What?"

I walked into the cat lounge and flopped onto the sofa. Tara, my sister Cassie, and our assistant, Willow, all followed. The three women stood staring at me like I'd lost my mind. Who knew, maybe I had.

"Maybe you should start at the beginning," Tara said.

I nodded. "I was at the cabin late this morning, trying to figure out what I was going to do about the ceremony, now that the church is closed for repair, when Siobhan came over to let me know she'd spoken to Finn, who'd informed her that Sally from the bakery had been found dead by her assistant this morning."

"Oh no. Poor Sally," Willow said. "What happened?"

"She was hit from behind with a rolling pin or a rolling-pin-shaped object. At least that's what Finn suspects."

"So get back to the part about Mrs. West," Cassie suggested.

"Finn told Siobhan it appeared as if Cody's mother might have been the last person to see Sally alive. It seems she went to the bakery late yesterday afternoon to change my cake order because, apparently, white cake with white frosting is boring and stupid."

I saw Tara cringe.

"Sorry." I cringed in response. "That was rude and very inappropriate. A woman is dead and here I am, complaining about the actions of the woman who might have killed her."

"Mrs. West might have killed her?" Tara asked, taking a seat next to Willow.

"Finn said two women were passing the bakery while Mrs. West was yelling at Sally. They heard her tell Sally to make the changes or suffer the consequences."

Willow audibly gasped. "You don't think she actually…"

"No. At least, I hope not. But the sheriff is taking the threat seriously. He told Finn to bring Mrs. West in for questioning. I think she's still there. I was told to stay far away from the place while the sheriff was on the island. And I did. For a while. But I got tired of waiting, so I decided to go by to take a peek. Finn saw me and yelled at me, so I came here."

"You know Sally was Sheriff Fowler's half sister?" Willow asked.

I frowned. "She was? I had no idea." I bit my lip. "I guess that's why Finn wanted me to stay out of the line of fire. He was just looking out for me."

"She and her husband moved to the island from Seattle to be closer to him," Willow confirmed. "I attend the same exercise class as Sally, and while I wouldn't say we were close, we chatted on several occasions. It sounds like Sally and her brother were pretty close."

"This sounds really bad," Tara said.

I had to agree.

"The sheriff must be devastated," Cassie said, a touch of sadness in her voice.

"Yeah," I agreed, feeling like a terrible person for trying to make Sally's death all about me.

"Do you think they're going to put Mrs. West in jail?" Cassie asked.

I narrowed my gaze. "I don't think based on an argument and nothing more they would actually arrest her."

"What if there's something more than just the argument?" Willow asked.

I really, really wished I could say without a doubt in my mind that Cody's mother would never get mad enough to haul off and smack someone with a rolling pin, but from her behavior in the past few days, I couldn't help but wonder if that wasn't exactly what she'd done.

******

While Sheriff Fowler didn't arrest Cody's mother, he did tell her that she was a person of interest in the investigation and warned her not to leave the island, which she wasn't planning to do anyway. His request still angered her. When Cody arrived at my cabin after dropping his mother at the inn, he looked as if he'd been put though the ringer. Poor guy. I couldn't imagine how I'd feel if my mother was the prime suspect in a murder investigation.

"Does it seem as if the sheriff actually thinks your mother is guilty of killing Sally?" I asked after opening a beer and handing it to the man I still hoped to marry in just a few days if we were able to find an alternate venue.

"He didn't say it in so many words, but Finn said in confidence that my mother was argumentative and even somewhat belligerent while being interviewed, which didn't help her case." Cody ran his hand through his hair. "I suspected my mother might not be quite as okay with our wedding plans as she indicated when I originally spoke to her. I even suspected a bit of an attitude, but I honestly didn't expect her to act the way she has."

"It does seem as if she's been trying to sabotage our wedding ever since she arrived on the island." I sighed, sitting down next to him. "I don't understand why. Doesn't she like me?"

Cody used one finger to tuck a stray strand of hair behind my ear. "She likes you. It's just that she blames you for ending my military career. I knew that and should have anticipated there was going to be fallout."

I sat up straight. "What? How can she blame me for ending your military career? I had nothing to do with that. We weren't even dating when you decided to leave the SEALs and move back to the island."

"I know." Cody let out a long breath. "It's just that she really had her heart set on my being career military, like my grandfather. And at one point I considered a career in the military as an option. But after a decade in the Navy, I realized that wasn't what I wanted for a lifetime. After moving back to the island and buying the newspaper, I had to explain my decisions to her. In the course of listing my reasons, I might have let it slip that one of them had to do with my feelings for you, and my desire to live in one place long enough to see where those feelings might lead."

I closed my eyes and groaned. And here I'd been thinking the only problem the woman had with me was my desire to get married on Madrona Island rather than in Florida. For the first time I understood that the loving, close mother-daughter relationship I'd hoped to have with Mrs. West had been doomed from the beginning.

Cody continued. "I'm sorry my mother is acting this way. I thought she'd have the maturity to behave herself at my wedding despite her feelings, but I can see now I was wrong. I don't believe she'd kill anyone, but I have no doubt she not only tried to sabotage our cake but that she yelled at the poor woman for hesitating to do what she demanded."

I couldn't help but throw my hands in the air. "So what do we do now? Do we cancel the wedding? For all we know, your mother could be in jail by Saturday."

"She isn't going to be in jail. We'll figure out who really killed Sally and my mother will be off the hook."

I began to pace. "We're getting married in four days. Four days!" I couldn't quite keep the screechy, loud tone out of my voice. "We don't have a venue for the ceremony or a cake. Your mother is not only the prime suspect in a murder investigation, but even if we manage to clear that up, she'll still hate me." I took a long breath in, then blew it out slowly. "Maybe this wedding just wasn't meant to be."

Cody put his hands on my shoulders. Turning me toward him, he looked me directly in the eyes. "Are you saying you want to cancel the wedding?"

I felt my anger dissipate as I looked into Cody's deep blue eyes. "No. That isn't what I want. I want to marry you and have your babies and build a life with you, but it seems as if things shouldn't be this hard."

"I know." Cody pulled me close and wrapped his arms around me. "But sometimes life is hard, and sometimes we're forced to make compromises. I wish you'd been able to have your dream wedding. I really do. But I know we make a good team. A strong team. If we work together, I know we can figure this out."

I squeezed Cody around the middle with my arms. "You're right. I'm sorry about the meltdown." I loosened my grip and took a step back and looked at Cody again. "What we need is a plan. A list. We have four days to pull everything together."

Cody kissed me on the nose. "That's my girl. I'll grab a pen and pad and we'll get to work."

I sat down on the sofa and stared into the cracking fire I'd built earlier to chase away the chill. Cody and I had real obstacles to overcome if we were going to get married on Saturday as planned, but if it took every ounce of energy I had, somehow I was going to make it happen.

"We have several small obstacles and one very large one," I said once Cody sat down next to me. "Beginning with what seemed like a huge obstacle this morning and now seems like a minor problem compared to Sally's murder: We need a place to hold the ceremony."

"What about here?" Cody asked. "The reception is going to be here on the estate, so why not just do the whole thing here?"

"What about the storm? We could cram everyone into the house for the reception if need be, but there won't be room to set up chairs for as many people as we ended up inviting."

"Yeah," Cody said. "The storm could be a problem. It's supposed to roll in tomorrow evening and the first wave should blow through by Friday morning, but according to the weather forecast, there should be a second wave blowing through shortly after that. If we're going to get married on Saturday, we need an indoor venue. Maybe the recreation center?"

I made a face. "That seems cold and impersonal. What would you think about postponing the wedding?"

"Until when?" he asked.

"Father Bartholomew is still waiting for the contractor to get back to him, but he hoped the church would be repaired in time to reopen on Sunday, November 25. If that happens, he offered to let us have the ceremony after the morning services. I know that isn't ideal, but we'll need to call everyone we invited anyway, so other than your mother and cousin, who came from out of town, I'm pretty sure everyone else will be able to come on the twenty-fifth."

"And if it doesn't reopen by then?"

"Then we'll need to move on to plan B, or maybe by that point it will be plan C. I know there's quite a bit of uncertainty involved at this point, but Father Bartholomew should have a better idea when the contractor will be done by the first part of next week. I'm inclined to wait to see what he comes back with."

Cody paused. From his frown, he wasn't happy with the idea, but eventually, he admitted that postponing the wedding to see if the church could still work out might be the best idea.

"So, about the cake…" Cody said.

"I'll ask Tara to make it. I should have asked her in the first place. I didn't want to make such a huge request because she's already going to be maid of honor and she's covering for me at the bookstore, but I kind of think she was hurt when I decided to order the cake from Sally."

"Okay." Cody jotted down a few notes. "We'll ask Father Bartholomew about doing the wedding at some point after the church reopens and Tara to do the cake. Are you still thinking of having the reception here at Finn and Siobhan's place?"

I nodded. "If it turns out to be nice by the time we get around to doing the ceremony, we'll have it in the yard, and if the weather is bad, we'll all cram into the house."

"Okay. Anything else?"

"It sounds like we have it covered, although it might be a good idea to find Sally's killer so your mom is no longer a suspect and we won't have that hanging over our heads."

"Let's call Father Bartholomew, then talk to Siobhan and Tara. Once we have those details ironed out, we can focus on proving she didn't kill Sally."

"Are you sure she didn't?" I asked.

"Of course I'm sure she didn't. I know she's been acting irrationally since she's been here, but she wouldn't attack anyone. At least I don't think she would."

"Has your mother always been this domineering?"

Cody shrugged. "She's the sort of person who likes to get her way. I know that's why my dad left. I suppose it's also why I went into the military. She had it in her head that I was going to have a career in the military, and she isn't the sort of person you say no to. I think she means well, but she does have a way of steamrolling over anyone who disagrees with her."

"Have you ever witnessed her taking out her frustration in a physical manner? Could she have been so frustrated that she hauled off and hit a woman who wouldn't do as she asked before she had a chance to think about the consequences?"

Cody frowned. "Honestly? I've seen her become physically aggressive. Not hit anyone, but she used to throw things at my dad. Dishes and knickknacks mostly." Cody groaned. "Maybe I was playing with fire to even invite her here. I'm beginning to think we should have eloped after all."

"I've been thinking the same thing."

Chapter 2

Thankfully, Father Bartholomew was happy to fit our ceremony in at some point after the church reopened, and Siobhan was fine with moving the reception to whatever date that might be. Tara was delighted to bake the cake, so all that was left to do was to prove Cody's mother didn't kill Sally so we didn't have her potential arrest looming over our heads. This, I decided, was going to be extra-hard because even Cody and I weren't certain she was innocent. All we could do was to proceed with the idea that she was innocent and hope we discovered someone else was guilty of the murder.

Siobhan suggested the sleuthing gang get together to come up with a plan to find Sally's killer. Our brothers, Danny and Aiden, had to work at the bar they'd recently purchased that evening, so it was Finn and Siobhan, Cody and me, and Tara and Cassie who met at my place, because Aunt Maggie and Michael were staying at Finn and Siobhan's and had offered to put their son, Connor, to bed. Siobhan had made snacks and set up the whiteboard in my living room. I could see she was anxious to get down to business and solve the crime. One of the things I loved most about my older sister was that she was an organized, take-charge sort of person. I guess that was what made her a good mayor as well.

"Let's start with the suspects and witnesses Sheriff Fowler has already identified and take it from there," she suggested, dry erase marker in hand.

"The sheriff has interviewed six people so far, including Mrs. West," Finn said. "He first spoke to Carla Hudson, Sally's assistant, who was the one who found Sally's body in the walk-in refrigerator this morning. While the bakery is open from nine to four every day, Sally usually arrived at eight and stayed until four, and Carla worked from seven to three. She helps with the baking in the morning, then leaves at three to pick up her daughter from her dance class. When she left yesterday, Sally was speaking to Mrs. West about the changes she wanted on the wedding cake. According to Carla, the conversation had turned into a shouting match by the time she left."

"So the bakery closed at four and Carla left at three. Do we know if anyone else came in between three and four?" I asked Finn.

"I'm not sure. I'd need to check with the sheriff. I do know Carla told him that the front door was unlocked when she arrived this morning, the cash was still in the cash drawer, and Sally was wearing the same clothes she'd had on the previous day, which led her to believe Sally was killed before she had a chance to lock up and cash out for the day. Carla said Sally was pretty rigid about closing at four because she had an exercise class she attended at five. Based on that, Carla is pretty sure Sally must have been killed between three o'clock, when she left, and four o'clock, when Sally would have locked the door and cashed out."

"And the witnesses who heard them arguing?" I asked. "What time was that?"

"Diane Grimes and Nicole Jenkins walked past the shop at around three thirty. Neither noted the exact time, but from their recollection of other stops they made, they estimate the time to be fairly accurate, give or take ten minutes. Both women saw a tall, heavyset woman with short, platinum hair shouting at Sally. They both remembered the woman wore tan slacks and a bright pink sweater. They didn't recognize her but said she was livid. They considered going in but decided Sally could take care of herself and walked on."

"So Mrs. West was in the shop yelling at Sally for thirty minutes?" I asked.

Finn shrugged. "Based on the eyewitness accounts, that seems to be the case. Of course, the women said give or take ten minutes, so it could have been closer to three twenty, and Carla might have been off by a few minutes too. Still, I think we should assume Mrs. West was on the premises for at least twenty minutes."

"I'm having a hard time believing anyone would be willing to put up with being yelled at for that long. Maybe the timeline is off somehow."

"Perhaps," Finn agreed. "The important thing is that Mrs. West was seen at the bakery and she was more than just a little irate."

I could see Cody's lips tighten. This had to be hard on him. Especially given his doubts about his mother's innocence. I wanted to help him and certainly didn't want to make things even harder. I needed to keep true to the purpose of the meeting and not fuss on timelines that seemed off.

"You must be right. Who else did the sheriff speak to?" I asked.

"After he spoke to Mrs. West, the sheriff interviewed Eric West, Cody's cousin. He'd been out drinking and wasn't even aware his Aunt Beverly had gone into town. He did say she'd been worked up about something when they had breakfast that morning, but she hadn't said what had her in a tizzy. As of now, the sheriff isn't considering any other suspects. At least not any I know of. He's aware of my relationship with Cody, and while he hasn't taken me off the case, I have the feeling he isn't sharing everything he knows with me."

"I assume he spoke to Sally's husband?" Siobhan said.

"He did. I don't know the outcome of that conversation, other than that Nick Enderling mentioned his wife had planned to have dinner with some friends from her exercise class the evening she died. I know the sheriff planned to call those friends to see if Sally had been in touch with any of them about being late or missing their dinner date altogether."

"We know Mrs. West was at the bakery at three o'clock, when Carla left for the day. If she'd been the one to kill Sally—and I'm certainly not saying she was—she would most likely have killed her before she left. We need to get a look at the bakery cash register log to find out if anyone stopped by to pick up an order or to make a purchase at any time after three o'clock," I said. "If anyone came after Mrs.

West left, an argument could be made that she wasn't the last person to see Sally alive."

"I'm assuming the sheriff has already taken the items in the cash drawer as well as the cash register tape," Siobhan said.

"I believe so," Finn said. "The crime scene guys were in the shop for most of the day. I doubt there's much left on the premises to find. I'll see whether I can find out if anyone came in after three."

"I think tracking down potential witnesses is important, but it sounds like the sheriff is already all over that. What he doesn't seem to be doing is coming up with an alternate list of suspects," Tara pointed out.

"Tara is right," Cassie said. "Maybe our time would be best spent figuring out who had motive to kill Sally."

"I guess we can start talking to people," Siobhan said.

"Willow told me that she attends the same exercise class Sally did. I'll talk to her to see if I can come up with a list of other attendees who might have been close to Sally," I said.

"It would make sense that Carla and Sally would chat while they work together all day. One of us should talk to Carla," Siobhan added.

"I'll do it," Tara offered. "I know her from a baking class we both took on San Juan Island a while back."

"And I'll talk to the other members of the chamber of commerce to see if anything was going on in that group," Siobhan offered. "It seems there's pretty much always one controversy or another with them."

"I'll talk to my mom to see if I can find out exactly what happened," Cody said. "It would give us a reference point if we had her timeline. She also might remember if anyone else came in while she was in the bakery."

"What can I do?" Cassie asked. "I'm the only one without a job."

"Why don't you talk to the owners or employees of the businesses on either side of the bakery?" I suggested. "Chances are, if things got that loud, they must have been disturbed by the noise."

"Let's all meet back here tomorrow after the bookstore closes," Siobhan said. "We can share what we found out then. If anyone finds a smoking gun they should, of course, call Finn right away."

Everyone agreed to the plan. We all chatted for a while longer and then everyone took off, leaving Cody and me alone. I hated the stress lines around his eyes and the tightness of his jaw. I was sure this had to be killing him. I wanted to help him deal with things, but I had no idea how to do it.

"I'm sorry," I said, tossing another log on the fire. "This must be awful for you."

Cody ran a hand through his thick brown hair. "It isn't fun."

"I know things look bad now, but I'm sure once we start to ask around, we'll find there are other suspects much more likely to have hit Sally with a rolling pin or something like it. Let's not forget that Danny was suspected of a murder only last month, and despite the evidence, he turned out to be completely innocent."

"I'm sure you're right."

I cringed just a bit at the tone of hopelessness in his voice. "I'm going to take Max out for a walk. Do you want to come?"

Cody nodded. "Yeah. I could use some air."

After bundling up against the cold night air, we headed out onto the beach. Cody took my hand in his as we walked along the waterline, where waves rolled gently onto the shore. The storm that was predicted hadn't arrived yet, so the billions of stars that were sprinkled across the night sky shone down on us as we made our way across the sandy beach. I figured Cody needed a break from talking about the wedding, his mother, and Sally's murder, so I decided to fill him in on the things I'd firmed up that day for the giant Thanksgiving feast we planned to hold at Mr. Parsons's house because we wouldn't be on the island for Christmas. At least I didn't think we would be. If Mrs. West did end up in jail, our Christmas trip to visit her in Florida would be off.

"I spoke to Francine today," I began. "She said the number of people coming to Mr. Parsons's dinner has passed seventy. She assures me that she and her group of volunteers have the food handled, but she suggested we might need to rent additional chairs and tables from an off-island vendor. She's already reserved every table and chair the one and only local rental company has, but she doesn't think that will be enough."

"I'll make some calls tomorrow. Danny and Aiden are closing the bar on Thanksgiving, so we could use some of their tables and chairs in a pinch, but it would be easier to rent what we need. I might be able to find a company to deliver them on Tuesday or Wednesday and then pick them up after the holiday weekend."

"The church will be closed. I bet we could borrow some chairs and tables from them if need be."

Cody paused and picked up a stick, which he tossed for Max. "I know this feast is a lot of work. With everything that's happened in regard to the wedding, it might be too much work. But Mr. Parsons is really looking forward to it."

"I'm happy we're doing this for him. Francine offered to take over the planning and cooking of the food, so it hasn't been all that much work for us at all."

Cody paused and looked out toward the sea. "It was really nice of her to pitch in."

"I think she gets lonely, and planning the party makes her feel included. She seems really excited, and Aunt Maggie, Siobhan, Tara, and even Summer are helping. Mr. Parsons has been strutting around like a sixty-year-old since the invitations went out. It's good to see him with so much energy and enthusiasm. And the best part is that everyone who usually has nowhere to go on Thanksgiving has been invited. This is good for all our friends. I'm happy we're in a position to spearhead things."

The breeze picked up slightly after we turned to walk back toward my cabin. Cody usually spent at least part of his nights with Mr. Parsons, but his friends Banjo and Summer had offered to spend the two weeks between the weekend before our wedding and the weekend after Thanksgiving at his house so we could have the time we needed first to prepare for the wedding and then to prepare for the Thanksgiving feast. We weren't taking a honeymoon now due to time constraints, but every day with Cody was like a honeymoon, so I didn't really mind. Or at least I hadn't. With everything that had been going on, I felt like I really did need a break.

"By the way," Cody said as we paused to allow Max to catch up with us after chasing something only he had seen, "I spoke to the contractor today. He spoke to the engineer, who verified that most of the walls we want to take out on the third floor of the house should be removable as long as we add a header and make a few modifications to our design."

I smiled. "That's great."

"He'd like to get started right after the first of the year. January is a slow time for him. I figured we could just stay in your cabin while the work is being done."

"And Mr. Parsons? We talked about how the noise and dust could affect his health."

"Francine volunteered to have him stay with her during the construction, and he said he was fine with that."

I raised a brow. "Really? That surprises me."

Cody took my hand and began to walk again. "Why? Mr. Parsons and Francine get along splendidly."

"True. I guess I'm just surprised he's okay with the disruption to his home and life. There was a time not all that long ago when he never would have gone for any of this."

Cody shrugged. "I guess he's mellowed."

I turned and looked at Cody. "He's more than mellowed. He's a totally different person since you moved in with him. You've changed his life."

"*We've* changed his life, and in many ways, he's changed ours." Cody paused. "I didn't have any strong male role models when I was younger. My father left when I was just a kid, and my mother's father didn't live near us. In a way, Mr. Parsons is like the grandfather I never had, and he's told me more than once that he considers me the son he never had." Cody looked at me. "And I know he adores you. You took care of him even before I came back to the island. We're a family. Maybe a different sort of family, but still a family. I think that's why he's willed his estate to us. He wants his family to continue after he's gone."

Cody was right; Mr. Parsons *was* family. "You know, I still haven't settled on someone to walk me down the aisle. I was thinking of asking Aiden, but how about if I ask Mr. Parsons? Aiden is already a groomsman."

He stopped walking. "Really? I'm sure that would mean a lot to him."

"He didn't come to mind right away, but you make a good point that he's like a grandfather to you. I'd be honored to have him be part of our special day."

Cody took my hand and started walking again. "We'll ask him tomorrow. And thank you. This means a lot to me."

I let out a small laugh. "Well, he *is* giving us a multimillion-dollar estate on which to raise our family."

Cody looped his arm around my neck. "True. But even if that wasn't the case, you'd ask him, because it's important to me."

I leaned my head on his shoulder. "You're right. I would. I want this day to be special for both of us."

We continued the trek to my cabin in silence. I had the wedding and the plans I still needed to finalize on my mind, as well as Sally's murder and the potential for real problems for Cody's mom. I was really sad we'd most likely never have the close relationship I'd hoped for, but I had other people in my life who loved me unconditionally, and that would be enough.

"It looks like the reinforcements have arrived," Cody said as we arrived at my deck to find a furry brown-striped cat waiting for us.

"I was hoping one of Tansy's cats would show up to help us find Sally's killer," I said as I walked forward and then bent over to pet the cat. I'm not sure exactly how it works, but every time I'd been tasked with solving a mystery in the past few years, a magical cat had shown up to steer me in the right direction. "What's your name, sweetie?"

"Meow."

"I don't speak cat, so I guess I'll need to call Tansy."

"It's late," Cody said.

I looked at my watch. "It's late, but not that late. If she's gone to bed, she most likely won't answer, and I'll leave a message and she can call me back in the morning." I glanced at Max. "Can you wipe his feet before he comes in? I want to make the call before it gets any later."

I kicked off my shoes and walked in stocking feet across the hardwood floor. The cabin was nice and warm from the fire we'd left burning. I really loved crisp nights such as this, when I could cuddle with Max, Cody, and one of Maggie's quilts.

I signed onto my cell and dialed Tansy's number.

"I guess Cosmo must have arrived," Tansy said upon answering.

"If Cosmo is a huge, furry brown cat, yes, he's arrived. He's really beautiful. And so cuddly-looking."

Tansy laughed. "Cosmo loves to cuddle, and he isn't just beautiful but special as well."

"Special how?" I asked.

"He is connected to the truth that lives within the lies. Follow his lead and you will find the answers you seek."

I'm not sure why, but Tansy's statement made me a little nervous. I wanted to ask what she meant by that, but I'd been working with Tansy long enough to know she wouldn't tell me, so I thanked her and hung up. When I returned to the deck, I found Cody holding Cosmo while Max lounged at his feet.

"So, is this a Tansy cat?" Cody asked

"It is. His name is Cosmo."

Cody smiled. "I'm very glad to meet you, Cosmo." He looked at me. "If a magical cat is here to help us find Sally's killer, that must mean my mom is innocent."

I frowned. I wasn't at all sure that was the case, but I didn't want Cody to worry. "Yes." I forced a smile. "I imagine that's exactly what his arrival means."

Chapter 3

Wednesday, November 14

"Cody's cousin Eric is a donkey butt."

"Donkey butt?" Tara laughed at my announcement.

I furrowed my brow as I tried to prevent my ire from taking an unladylike turn. "I have a much harsher name in mind, but with everything that's happened this past week, I figure I must have negative karma at work. I want things to go smoothly from this point forward, so I'm trying to keep my soul clean and my aura pure."

"I see." Tara suppressed a laugh. "So, is Eric a donkey butt based on a general assessment or did he do something specific?"

"He did something specific."

Tara flinched. "What did he do now?"

I curled my hands into fists as I attempted to contain my rage. "He punched Finn square in the face. The whole thing was totally unprovoked." I let out a groan. "What an idiot. Not only is Finn bigger and stronger than Eric, and therefore totally capable of flattening the guy, but Finn is a cop. He could have both flattened him and arrested him."

"I'm assuming he didn't do either," Tara said in a gentle voice I knew was intended to help calm me down.

"No," I moaned. "Finn didn't want to create any more problems for Cody, so he gave him a strong talking-to, then took him back to the inn and told him to sleep it off."

Tara walked over and gave me a hug. "Okay, so Eric punched Finn. Why would he do that?"

"I found out this morning that Eric showed up at Finn and Siobhan's house last night after they got home from the Scooby meeting. When Finn answered the door, Eric didn't say a word; he just punched him. Finn managed to pin him to the ground, but all Eric would say was that he was defending his aunt's honor after Finn manhandled her that afternoon."

"Manhandled?" Tara asked.

"Finn had to pick her up for questioning. Cody's mom was less than cooperative, apparently, so he had to forcefully escort her to the back seat of his squad car. How on earth did we get to the point where my brother-in-law has to take my fiancée's mother into custody for questioning a few days before my wedding? Or at least a few days before my wedding was supposed to take place. Who knows when it will take place at this point."

Tara put her arm around my shoulders. "It does seem you've had more than your share of problems with this wedding. But I'm sure things will eventually come together, and then you and Cody can put this whole fiasco behind you."

"Sure, unless Cody's mom ends up in prison. Then what? Do we take the kids to the big house to visit Grandma?"

Tara raised a brow. "I know you're upset, but I think you might be overreacting just a bit. I'm sure we'll find Sally's real killer and the whole nightmare will come to an end."

I lowered my voice and leaned in close. "What if she *is* the real killer?"

"Why would you say that?"

I shrugged. "The woman has been a loose cannon ever since she's been here. And I spoke to Tansy last night, after my latest kitty sidekick showed up, and she said something about a truth at the source of every lie. I just have this feeling the truth we find might not be the one we're hoping for."

Tara let out a long breath. "I guess all you can do is follow the truth, no matter where it leads."

Tara was right. If Cody's mother did kill Sally, she would need to pay the price for her actions. I wasn't sure how Cody would deal with that, but I'd be there with him. If she was innocent, we'd prove it and she could get on with her life. We could all get on with our lives.

"Do you want some coffee?" Tara offered.

"No. I have errands to do."

"Errands or sleuthing?"

"Sleuthing. I'd like to have something concrete to bring to the meeting tonight. Something other than a sick feeling that Mrs. West may actually be guilty, as the sheriff suspects."

"I'm sure she didn't kill Sally."

I sighed. "Let's hope not."

I left Coffee Cat Books and headed to the north shore, where Willow Wood lived with her son, Barrington Wood Turner, and her best friend and parenting partner, Alex Turner. She worked for us part-time but wasn't scheduled to be in today. I'd called ahead and she'd indicated she'd be happy to discuss whatever I wanted. I hadn't seen Barrington for quite a while, so I was anxious to see how big he'd gotten too. He was only a few months older than Connor but had been a larger baby at birth and had demonstrated an exceptional rate of learning even in infancy. Knowing as I did that he would grow up to do exceptional things that would save lives felt weird to me, especially because Alex and Willow had no idea about it, but Tansy had explained it was important to keep it a secret.

"Thank you for seeing me," I said after I knocked on her door and Willow invited me in.

"Come on back. The baby is in the sunroom with Alex. It's been a while since you've seen him."

"Is he still talking a mile a minute?"

"He is. Mostly just babbles, but every now and then I feel like he's trying to make a point."

"He does seem like a very intelligent baby."

"Oh, he is," Willow said. "Of course, I'm sure all parents say that."

I greeted Alex and fussed over Barrington for a few minutes, and then Alex took Barry up to his room so Willow and I could chat. I briefly explained the situation with Cody's mother and that we were trying to find out all we could about Sally, her friends and enemies, and life in general in the weeks before her death. "You mentioned you attended the same exercise class as Sally, and we heard she planned to have dinner with a few people from there the night she died. We want to speak to those friends, and I hoped you knew who they were."

Willow furrowed her brow. "I don't know who she planned to have dinner with, but she seemed to be friends with Connie Salisman, Eve Donner, and Lisa Kinder. I've overheard them discussing getting together after class on more than one occasion."

I jotted down the names. "Is there anyone in class she might have been having problems with?"

"Silvia Hill," Willow answered at once. "Silvia served on the chamber of commerce with Sally. I don't know what the problem was between them, but I've seen them talking in the parking lot either before or after class. I could never hear what they were saying, but from body language, it looked as if their conversations were heated."

I jotted down Silvia's name. "Does anyone else come to mind?"

Willow shook her head. "Not really. Although Sally and I attended the same class, we weren't friends. We'd say hi if we passed in the hallway or parking lot, but that was about it. If Sally was tight with anyone other than the three I mentioned, I didn't notice, although one of them might be able to tell you about other friends she had."

"Okay, I'll track down Connie, Eve, and Lisa. Siobhan was going to follow up with the chamber of commerce members, so I'll mention Silvia to her. If you think of anyone else, call me."

"I will. I'm working tomorrow, so you can find me at the store if you have additional questions. You have so much on your plate right now. If I can help you in any way, I'd like to. Barry and I can never repay you for all you've done for us."

"I was happy to do it." I looked around the bright, sunny room. Last year at this time, Willow was pregnant and homeless. "I'm very happy things worked out for all of you."

I left the house Alex owned and Willow lived in and drove into town. Cody had been quiet this morning, so I thought I'd stop by the newspaper to see if there was anything I could do to cheer him up. I hoped he'd been able to talk to his mother and that it had gone smoothly. As it turned out, smoothly was the exact opposite of what had occurred.

"What do you mean, she tried to get on the ferry?" I asked.

"I guess she didn't feel the need to follow the sheriff's instructions to stay on the island and decided to go shopping in Seattle. Or at least that's what she said. She had her luggage in the trunk of her car, so I'm pretty sure she was really going home."

"Oh, Cody. That's going to make her look guilty."

"I know. And she should have realized the sheriff would take precautions. As I could have predicted, her name and photo had been provided to the folks who work for the ferry system and she was detained. Finn was forced to pick her up and hold her at his office until the sheriff could show up and talk to her. I don't know what's going to happen now, but there was talk of locking her up if she refused to cooperate."

"Was Eric with her?"

Cody let out a long sigh. "No. Maybe Mom really was just going shopping. It doesn't explain her luggage in the trunk, but she might have an explanation. I haven't been able to speak to her, so I have no idea what she was thinking. Finn said he'd try to arrange it so I can talk to her. He had no idea when we spoke what the sheriff was going to do."

"Can he lock her up if he doesn't have proof she killed Sally?"

Cody shrugged. "Maybe for a while. He'd need to charge her with something to keep her for long. Unless he has something we don't know about, it's likely he'll let her return to the inn with a stern warning about what will happen if she tries to leave again."

I walked across the room and wrapped my arms around him. I felt helpless to make this easier for him. Tansy said to follow the truth, which was exactly what I intended to do, but I was afraid where the truth might lead.

Cody had some work to finish up, so I decided to go back to the cabin and have a heart to heart with Cosmo. If he'd been sent to help me find the truth, we needed to get started. By the time the cat had shown up last night it was time to go to bed, and I'd gotten up early this morning to see Cody off and then gone into town myself to talk to Tara and see Willow. Some of the cats Tansy sent to me were gung ho to get right to work, while others took their time getting warmed up. I hadn't had a chance to get a feel for Cosmo's style, but given the tight timeline, I hoped he was as raring to go as I was.

The sky darkened as the day progressed. I could see the major storm that had been predicted was most likely going to show up before we met tonight. Cody planned to buy some pizzas for our shared dinner, and we had stocked up on beer the last time we'd gone to the market, so I figured I could use the time I had before the others arrived to work with Cosmo in the hope he could help me turn up a clue or two.

When I arrived at the cabin, I found Cosmo curled up with Max. Both were on Max's dog bed, which I'd left in front of the sliding door where the sun, if there had been any, would have come in, providing warmth.

"Hey, guys," I said after tossing the backpack I used as a purse onto the sofa. "We have work to do, so I hope you're all rested up."

Max barked once and Cosmo stretched and yawned. I supposed the first thing I should do was to take Max out for a bathroom break, which I did while Cosmo used the litter box and chowed down on the cat food I'd left for him that morning but he'd yet to eat.

The wind had picked up as the storm neared. The sky had turned a muddy gray color, which gave an eerie feel to the atmosphere. I pulled my sweatshirt around my middle as I walked along the beach with Max. The moody sky was congruent with the completely illogical behavior Mrs. West had been exhibiting since she'd been on the island. Danny and Cody had been friends when he'd been in high school while I hadn't been, so I hadn't hung out at his house and gotten to know his mother. She'd attended St. Patrick's, but she was an adult and I was a kid, so it wasn't like we'd ever talked or anything. I remembered her as being somewhat stern. There was some ruckus about a difference of opinion with the leader of the women's bible study group. I didn't remember a lot about it, just my mom mentioning that it seemed Mrs. West had never learned how to play nice with others. Danny had hung out at Cody's house when they were kids. He might have additional insight as to her behavior back then.

Not that it really mattered now or had any relevance to what was going on today. No matter her behavior years ago, there was no doubt about the fact that she'd been a time bomb waiting to go off since she'd been on the island now. Or maybe she'd already gone off. I just hoped she didn't have more than one explosion inside her.

As Max and I returned to the cabin it was starting to sprinkle. I wasn't sure exactly how to activate Cosmo, so I decided to sit down and have a chat with him. I tossed a log and some paper into the fireplace and lit a match. It was damp and chilly and the fire would take the chill out of the air.

"Okay, kitty," I said, curling up on the sofa with Cosmo and a quilt Maggie had made several years ago. "I know you're here to help, and I know the kitties that come my way usually have their own timeline, but I'm getting married in just three days—well, more like ten days, but still, I'd like to have this wrapped up sooner rather than later. Can we can get started?"

The cat started to purr, then head butted me under my chin in a show of affection. "Yes, I love you too," I said, scratching him behind the ears. "But we need to work now. We can cuddle later."

Cosmo rubbed against my chest a few times, then jumped to the floor. I watched and waited to respond to whatever cue he might provide. He headed over to a newspaper Cody had left on the kitchen counter. It was today's edition; the newspaper came out every

Wednesday, which was why Cody had to go into work despite all hell breaking loose.

"The newspaper? You want me to see something in it?"

"Meow."

I picked it up. "Okay. Which page?" I pointed to the front page. "This page?"

The cat didn't respond.

I turned to page two and three and pointed to each in turn. He still didn't respond. It wasn't until the double-page spread of six and seven that he let out a meow. I studied the pages, which featured a few small articles but mostly ads and the community announcements. On page six was an ad for the upcoming Christmas Festival, an article in the series Cody had been writing about the history of land acquisition from the time the island's founding fathers divided things up into twelve shares through current land ownership patterns, a related article about the church that had been built more than a century ago by the founding fathers but had recently burned to the ground as the result of arson, and an ad several local merchants had gone in on about upcoming Black Friday deals: Miranda Wells's store, Trinkets and Treasures; Banjo and Summer's shop, Ship Wreck Art and Novelties; Bella and Tansy's shop, Herbalities; the shop established by Maggie and Marley but currently run by Marley, Bait and Stitch; a T-shirt shop owned by our friend Valerie, Madrona Island Gifts; and Coffee Cat Books. I guess Tara must have taken care of that. She was the one in charge of ads. There was also a coupon for 20 percent off at the Driftwood Café.

On page seven, under the headline Community Announcements, was a paragraph letting everyone know that St. Patrick's would be closed until further notice due to the electrical fire; a reminder that the chamber of commerce wouldn't meet next week as they did most months on the fourth Thursday because of the holiday; a call for actors for the annual Christmas play put on by the community theater; a reminder that the community would hold their annual Thanksgiving food drive on Monday of next week so the canned goods and nonperishable items could be distributed on Wednesday; and a schedule of upcoming events for the holiday season.

Interestingly enough, also on page seven was an ad for Sally's Bakeshop, with a photo of their annual Christmas cake and instructions on ordering it, and an ad for Madrona Island Baked Goods, announcing a huge sale to commemorate the unveiling of their design for *their* annual Christmas cake on the Monday following Thanksgiving, as had been their holiday tradition for more than thirty years. The rivalry between Sally and Devita Colter, the owner of Madrona Island Baked Goods, was a fierce one, culminating in the annual Christmas cake each bakery offered. Madrona Island Baked Goods had been the only full-service bakery on the island for many years, until Sally moved here and began to siphon off a significant percentage of Devita's business. I'd always liked Devita, but the truth of the matter was, Sally offered a superior product, which was why I'd decided to go to her for my wedding cake.

I figured half the people and businesses on the island had been referred to in one way or another between the two newspaper pages, making the clue all but worthless. Still, after taking another look, I decided the item the cat wanted me to see was either the announcement about the chamber of commerce meeting or the ads for the Christmas cakes. It's crazy that Christmas cakes could lead to murder, but as I said, the rivalry was fierce. Of course, the number one motive when you took into account the items on the pages had to be the notice about the chamber meeting. Siobhan had said the board was a volatile group, which corresponded to bits of gossip I'd picked up lately. Maybe she'd have news that would lead to a motive by the time we met that evening.

Chapter 4

After we'd gathered and shared beer and pizza, we congregated around the whiteboard, which Siobhan had taken care of setting up. She started by asking Finn to share with us what he could.

"First, I've confirmed that Sheriff Fowler hasn't arrested Mrs. West for trying to leave the island. He deposited her back at the inn with a stern warning to stay put or end up in jail."

"Is she still the prime suspect in Sally's murder?" Tara asked.

"I believe so," Finn said. "The sheriff has spoken to several merchants nearby, all of whom reported that there were sounds of a commotion coming from the bakery on the day Sally was murdered."

"Didn't any of the other merchants think to head over to the bakery to check things out?" I asked.

"Apparently not," Finn said.

"I spoke to the merchants on either side of the bakery today," Cassie said. "On the north side is a novelty store specializing in souvenirs and local art. The owner, Miranda Wells, told me that she heard the noise and went out to the sidewalk and peeked in the window of the bakery. She saw a woman she later identified as Mrs. West pounding on the counter, but Sally seemed to have the situation under control, and a group from the ferry walked into her store, so she returned to help her customers."

"I have an interesting sidenote relating to the souvenir shop before we move on," Tara said.

"And what's that?" Siobhan asked.

"When I spoke to Carla today, she informed me that Sally and Miranda Wells had been at war over retail space. It seems Miranda's lease is up for renewal and Sally approached the owner of the building that houses the bakery, Miranda's place, and two other businesses, about taking over the lease for Miranda's shop."

"Why?" I asked.

"Sally wanted to expand so she could offer indoor seating. She was interested in opening a tea shop and was thinking of knocking out the wall dividing the bakery from Miranda's trinket shop."

"Seems like that might give Miranda a motive for murder," Cody said.

Cassie nodded. "Carla didn't say that in so many words, but she admitted there was no love lost between the women. I'm not surprised Miranda didn't help Sally even if she did suspect she was in danger."

Siobhan wrote the name *Miranda Wells* on the whiteboard. "What about the merchant south of the bakery?"

"That's a dry cleaner. The owner, Oliver Patton, said he didn't hear much yesterday. It's noisy in his shop with the machines going, so I could see why he might not have realized there was a murder taking place next door. I also spoke to the business directly across the street, but no one admitted to have heard or seen anything unusual."

Siobhan added the names of everyone Cassie had spoken to on the whiteboard. Then she turned to Tara. "You said you spoke to Carla. Did she say anything else we don't already know?"

"Actually she did," Tara said. "When Carla arrived in the morning and saw the cash drawer hadn't been closed out the previous day, she ran the tape so any sales recorded from that point on would be recorded to the correct date. She didn't have time to reconcile the previous day's receipts because she needed to see to the baking, so she put the register receipt and the money into a bank bag. She wasn't aware at that point that Sally was dead and figured she could reconcile it when she came in."

"Did Carla notice anything interesting about the cash register tape or the money in the drawer?" Siobhan asked.

"She saw that the last item to be rung up was at three fifty-five. Based on the dollar amount, she assumed the final purchase for the day was for a dozen cookies."

My eyes grew wide. "So if someone came in to buy cookies at three fifty-five and Cody's mom was already gone by then, that might prove she wasn't the last person to see her alive."

"Perhaps," Tara replied. "The problem is, according to the register tape, the purchase was made with cash, which means there's no way to know who bought the cookies unless someone saw the customer or they come forward."

"Maybe someone will come forward once the news of Sally's death gets out," I said with a hint of hope in my voice.

Siobhan looked at Finn. "Before we move on, do you have anything to add?"

"Just that the sheriff seems to be waiting for something from the crime lab. I have the feeling that whatever it is could either prove Mrs. West's guilt or innocence. I'll keep my ear to the ground."

Siobhan looked at me. "Cait, do you have anything?"

I nodded. "I spoke to Willow about the women Sally was most likely to hang out with during her exercise class. She identified Connie Salisman, Eve Donner, and Lisa Kinder. I haven't had a chance to follow up with them yet, but I will."

Siobhan noted the three names on the board.

"I also had a chat with Cosmo today," I continued. I explained about the cat who'd shown up last night, as well as the page in the newspaper he'd pointed me to. "There were a lot of businesses as well as individuals mentioned between the two pages, but it seems to me out of all the items, the announcement about the chamber of commerce meeting is probably the clue Cosmo wanted me to find."

"I agree the chamber is a good lead," Siobhan said. "I spoke to several chamber members today, including Silvia Hill. It seems there's a proposal before the board to start charging an annual fee to all chamber members that would be used to promote the island businesses to tourists who come over on the ferry. Arguments between the chamber members have become quite heated. On the pro side are the members who feel a focused advertising campaign in places like Seattle would be good for the economy of the entire island, but there are members who argue that not all businesses on the island have chosen to join the chamber, and it's likely those businesses would prosper thanks to the campaign, even though they wouldn't have paid anything toward it. The folks on the con side, including Sally, think the fee should be waged as a tax that would be handled by the island council, not the chamber."

"So that everyone who has a business on the island would be taxed, not just those who are members of the chamber," I clarified.

"Exactly," Siobhan said.

"Seems like a good idea to me. I wouldn't want to be forced to pay a fee for advertising that would benefit the entire island but would only be assessed on those of us who belong to the chamber."

"Most of the members who've been voting against the proposal feel as you do. Those who have been voting to approve the fee argue that if the island council gets involved and creates a tax for this purpose, they'll also control how that money is spent. Those who support the fee at the chamber level but oppose a tax want to be assured that the money earmarked for this project will go to this project." Siobhan paused, then continued. "The chamber members who are against getting the island council involved aren't wrong to be concerned. I've seen taxes levied at the local level with the intention of earmarking it for a specific purpose wind up being spent on something else."

"Can the council do that?" I asked.

"They can," Siobhan answered. "Most local tax initiatives are worded very loosely. If a tax is earmarked for promotion, it could be argued that paying for a new statue for the harbor or painting all the streetlights on Main or even repairing roads is promoting prosperity for the island, so the money collected from the tax might be used for those things, even though it was originally intended to be used for advertising. I'm not saying that would happen, but it's possible."

"While this is all very interesting, why would this debate lead to Sally's death?" Cody asked. "Identifying her killer is the purpose of this discussion and I feel we're getting sidetracked."

"Sorry," Siobhan said. "I do have a point with all this. First, it looks like the majority of the members support the fee and oppose getting the island council involved. Sally was very much opposed to the fee and had been leading a movement to found a second chamber of commerce, giving folks who want to enjoy the benefits of such a group but don't want to be forced to pay the fee a place to go. Keep in mind, the initiative on the table involves charging a marketing fee to current chamber members, and to current chamber members only. If the initiative passes and a bunch of businesses secede and move over to a new group, they won't be charged the fee that will be levied by a body they no longer are part of."

"Do you actually think someone would kill Sally over this second chamber idea?" Cody asked.

Siobhan shrugged. "Maybe not, but it's led to some heated debates. It sounds, from what I've heard, like Sally was probably killed in a fit of rage. The executive director of the chamber of commerce, Eli Alderman, has been very vocal about the danger in dividing what's now a fairly powerful group that has been successful in promoting its members, into what would become two weak and ineffective ones. Additionally, his job is on the line. His salary is paid from chamber dues. If the chamber is divided, there's a good chance the membership that's left wouldn't be able to pay that salary."

"Would you say that now that Sally's dead, the idea of a second group will die as well?" I asked.

"Actually, I do. Founding an organization such as a chamber of commerce is very labor intensive. Sally seemed to have both the vision and the desire to make it happen. If you ask me, there isn't anyone else who cares enough to jump through all the hoops required, so now that Sally is dead, the idea will fizzle out."

The room fell silent. I supposed that there would be those, such as Eli Alderman, who would benefit from Sally's death. Of course, if someone from the chamber of commerce, like Eli, did kill Sally, I had no idea how we'd prove it.

Finally, Siobhan spoke again. "So, we've identified two new suspects. Sally was threatening to take over the lease currently held by Miranda Wells, which I imagine could very well put her out of business. Miranda was in her shop next door to Sally's bakery at the time she died, giving her both motive and opportunity. Eli Alderman's job was being threatened by Sally's campaign to start a second chamber of commerce to avoid the fee the current one wants to assess on its members. I suppose there are other proponents of the fee who could benefit from Sally's death as well." Siobhan paused. "Do we have any other suspects to discuss?"

"I wonder what happens to Sally's bakery now that she's dead." I said. "Will it close? Will Carla continue to run it? Did someone else inherit it who might take over?"

"Good question." Siobhan wrote *heir to bakery* on the whiteboard.

"Sally only had one competitor," I said. "Madrona Island Baked Goods had been operating on the island for more than thirty years. When Sally arrived here four years ago, she managed to steal a lot of customers from Madrona Island Baked Goods. If Sally's bakery ends up closing, it will benefit Madrona Island Baked Goods quite a bit."

"That's a good point." Siobhan wrote *Devita Colter*, the owner Madrona Island Baked Goods, on the whiteboard.

"Of course, Devita is a tiny little thing and sixty years old if she's a day," Tara pointed out. "I doubt she cracked Sally's head open with a rolling pin."

"True," I admitted. "I suppose she could have had someone kill Sally on her behalf, but I doubt it. Devita seems like a nice woman who wouldn't hurt a fly. I'm just looking to identify anyone who will benefit from Sally's death." I looked at Cody. "Did you ever have the chance to talk to your mother?"

"No. By the time I went over to the inn, she was in custody for trying to leave the island. I went by again on my way home this afternoon, but she didn't answer her door. I knocked on the door of Eric's room, and he told me that she'd taken a sleeping pill and gone to bed. I'll try again tomorrow."

Siobhan looked at the whiteboard. "It looks like we have a starting place. I suggest we try to narrow things down a bit by the time we meet again tomorrow night. Cait has three of Sally's friends to speak to and Cody is going to talk to his mother. I have a few ideas I want to follow up on as well, so let's call it a night."

Tara stood up. "The rain is starting to come down hard, so I'm going to take off. I'll be at the bookstore tomorrow if anyone needs me to do anything."

After Tara left, Finn, Siobhan, and Cassie went back to the big house, leaving Cody and me alone for the first time since that morning. "Are you doing okay?" I asked.

"Not really."

"I understand that. Is there anything I can do?"

Cody shook his head. "At least nothing you aren't already doing. I keep thinking that someone else will begin to stand out as a real suspect, but if I had to bet on the killer at this moment, I'd have no choice but to put my money on my mother. I hate that I think she might actually be guilty."

"We've identified others," I said.

"Maybe."

"Is there something else?" I asked.

Cody hesitated before he answered. "I did hear something today I didn't mention just now."

I raised a brow. "What did you hear?"

"When I spoke to Eric this afternoon, he told me that he's sure my mother is guilty. He went into her room last night to get the shampoo she'd borrowed from him because she'd forgotten hers. Mom had already taken her sleeping pill and gone to bed, but she'd left the connecting door unlocked, so he tiptoed into her bathroom. He found her clothes on the floor. Tan slacks and a pink sweater. He picked them up to toss them into a dirty clothes bag and noticed something red on them. He was sure it was blood."

"Oh, Cody. What are you going to do?"

He ran his hands through his hair. "I don't know. I asked Eric for the clothes so I could evaluate the stain myself, but he said he'd already disposed of them. I told him that he could end up in trouble for disposing of evidence, and he argued that he felt he had no choice and that no one would ever know. He said he wasn't going to tell anyone and assumed I wouldn't tell either. When I responded that I might very well do just that, he laughed and pointed out that the clothes and therefore the evidence were gone, and if he was asked about it, he'd deny he'd ever seen them."

"Why would Eric cover for your mom? I hardly know him, but he doesn't seem like the sort to cover for anyone."

"I think my mom has been supporting him. She brought him on this trip, and she mentioned at one point that he'd been living in her basement. He doesn't have a job or a lot of prospects. He must figure if she goes to prison, that will be the end of the gravy train."

"We need to tell Finn," I said.

"No," Cody responded. "Not yet. I'm going to talk to my mom in the morning. I want to hear what she has to say and then decide what to do. If she killed Sally, she'll need to pay the cost, but now all I have is Eric's word that Mom's clothes had blood on them. For all I know, he's lying."

"Why would he lie?"

"That's what he does. That's what he's done his whole life. He's a cheat and a liar and the entire family, with the exception of my mother apparently, knows it."

"Okay, but why would he lie about this?"

Cody shrugged. "Maybe he figured there might be something in it for him. Maybe he figured if I thought he had something damaging on my mother, I'd be willing to pay him to keep it quiet. There's no telling why he does what he does, but he can't be trusted."

I supposed Cody's theory on a potential blackmail scheme could be true, but I sort of doubted it. As I've said more than once since I met him, Eric is a grade-one donkey butt. He's opinionated and annoying and seems to act impulsively, without considering the consequences. He drinks too much and appears to have zero ambition. He most certainly isn't the sort of person I'd ever want to have a relationship with, but he did seem to care about Mrs. West. And I didn't think it was just the gravy train thing Cody mentioned. From what I'd seen, it seemed he had a genuine affection for Cody's mom. If the family really had shunned him with the exception of her, I supposed I could understand why he might hold her in high regard.

Chapter 5

Thursday, November 15

When Cody and I decided to get married in November, I knew the wedding was going to be somewhat hectic given the shortness of time, but I had no idea I'd be spending my last days as a single woman trying to keep my future mother-in-law out of prison.

I glanced out the window at the pouring rain. The storm had arrived as predicted, and the gloominess matched my mood. Cody had left after breakfast to see his mom. Hopefully, she'd have something to share that would shed light on what had happened on Monday afternoon. In the meantime, I planned to go into town to speak to Sally's friends: Connie Salisman, Eve Donner, and Lisa Kinder. I hoped one of them could tell me something that could reveal who had really killed Sally. I just wanted to be pointed anywhere other than Cody's mother.

Lisa Kinder worked at the library on Tuesdays and Thursdays, so I arranged to meet her there. She was manning the front desk, so she couldn't get away, but with the pouring rain, the entire town was deserted, including the library. I knew Lisa fairly well because the bookstore and the library often held events in cooperation with each other. The readathon we'd sponsored last summer was one example.

"Morning, Lisa. Thank you for agreeing to see me."

"No problem. Anything I can do to help put Sally's killer behind bars. I still can't believe she's gone."

I shook the rain from my slicker and walked up to the counter. "It's been quite a shock. I just spoke to her last week about my wedding cake. I'm having a hard time wrapping my head around the whole thing."

"I take it you're helping Finn, as you often do."

I nodded, sending moisture from my hair onto the floor. "I am. In a way. I'm mostly just talking to people who knew Sally. On the surface, it doesn't seem there's a clear suspect. Do you have any idea who would want to hurt Sally?"

Lisa paused and tilted her head. "I don't know for certain, but I heard from Carla that there was a customer who wasn't happy with her order and went all Rambo on poor Sally. Carla seemed confident it would turn out this woman was the killer. Seems ridiculous to me to get so angry over a cake."

I decided not to mention I was about to become related to this woman. "I agree. It is ridiculous. I know both Finn and Sheriff Fowler have spoken to the customer who was so upset the afternoon Sally died. I agree she makes a good suspect, but she's far from being the only one. I'm talking to Sally's friends to see if anyone knows of someone who might not make quite as obvious a suspect but should still be considered. It seems to me to be a good idea to have all bases covered."

"Yeah, I can see that." Lisa tapped her chin. "I wasn't exactly best friends with Sally. We were really just exercise buddies. There's a group of us who all take the same class, and sometimes we meet afterward for drinks or dinner. Sally would join us at times, but she didn't seem to be making the effort as often lately. The popular opinion was that she hadn't been going out with us so much because she was seeing someone on the side while her husband was away from home so often."

"Sally was having an affair?"

"I don't know it for a fact, but she was complaining her husband was never around. His business is in Seattle, you know. I guess when Sally first expressed a desire to move to Madrona and open up a bakery, her husband said he could work from home a good part of the time. According to Sally, it didn't work out that way. She told the group on more than one occasion that things weren't going as planned and one of them was going to have to make a change in their career if the marriage was going to last. It seemed clear it was Sally's intention that her husband be the one to make the change. And from what she said to us, it seemed he was considering it. Then his mother got sick. He was trying to do his part in helping his siblings to care for her, so apparently, he was flying back and forth between coasts to pitch in. I think the idea of him selling his business was put on the back burner with things already so hectic."

"So where does the affair fit into that?" I asked a bit impatiently.

"Hang on. I'm getting to that." Lisa rested her elbows on the counter, leaned in, and lowered her voice. "Anyway, a few weeks ago, another woman in the exercise group, Beth Bennington, said she saw Sally with a man at a restaurant on San Juan Island. She'd never seen Sally's husband and assumed from the lovey-dovey looks they were giving each other that it was him, home from taking care of his mother. When she described him to us, however, I knew immediately the man wasn't Sally's husband."

"Had you ever seen Sally's husband?"

Lisa nodded. "He picked her up from class once when her car was in the shop. He was tall, thin, and blond. Beth described this man as dark-haired with olive skin, maybe Italian. There was no way that man was the same one I saw."

"And you're sure he couldn't have been a friend or a customer?"

Lisa shrugged. "I didn't see them together, but Beth said they looked to be intimate."

An affair made a good motive for a murder. Maybe the husband found out about it and killed his cheating wife. Or maybe the Italian lover wanted to end things and Sally wouldn't let him go. Maybe she threatened to tell his wife, assuming he had one. There were any number of reasons an affair could lead to murder. I needed to check out this lead further. "Do you happen to know the restaurant where Beth saw them?"

"She didn't say. I guess you can ask her. I don't have her contact information with me now. If you aren't able to track her down, you might ask Eve

Donner. She seemed to know more about what might have been going on with Sally and this mystery guy than the rest of us. In fact, I had a feeling she suspected who he was, though she didn't name him."

"Do you know where I can find Eve?"

"She works at the Driftwood Café. She should be there today."

"Okay, and thank you. Is there anything else you can think of before I go?"

Lisa drummed her nails on the counter. "Not really. Sally was an intense person. She seemed to need to be busy all the time. She had her own business, she attended exercise class at least four times a week, she was on the board of the chamber of commerce, and I'm pretty sure she was involved in community theater too. She knew a lot of people, but I didn't have the sense she had a lot of friends. I almost felt bad for her. I hope you figure out who killed her. She didn't deserve to die."

No, she really didn't. I left the library and headed toward the Driftwood Café.

The idea that Sally might have had a guy on the side intrigued me. I needed to find someone, anyone, who made a better suspect than Cody's mother, and a secret lover provided me with a good candidate. When I arrived at the café, Cosmo was sitting near the door under the awning.

I parked, walked over, and picked him up. "What are you doing here?"

"Meow."

"Even a better question, how did you get here in the rain? You aren't even wet."

"Meow."

"I see. Well, the Driftwood doesn't allow animals inside. Wait for me in the car. I'll only be a few minutes."

I deposited the cat inside, then went back toward the café. "Morning, Kimmy," I said to the hostess after shaking the moisture from my umbrella and folding it into the dry sleeve I kept in my backpack. "Is Eve Donner working today?"

"Yeah. She's waiting tables in the back."

"I need to talk to her. I could use some hot tea and maybe a muffin. If you have a table in Eve's section, you can just seat me and she can come over to talk to me when she has a minute."

"That shouldn't be a problem. It's been really slow today with all the rain."

After I was seated, Kimmy grabbed me a cup of tea, then told Eve I wanted a muffin and a few minutes of her time. I watched as Eve nodded and waved at me. A few minutes later, she showed up at my table with a warm pumpkin nut muffin.

"You wanted to speak to me?" Eve asked.

"If you have a minute. I have some questions about Sally Enderling's death. I understand you were friends."

Eve slid into the booth across from me. "We were friends of a sort. We attended the same exercise class and went out for a meal every now and then."

"I spoke to Lisa Kinder, who told me about Beth Bennington having seen Sally at a restaurant on San Juan Island with a man who wasn't her husband. She suggested you might know who he was."

Eve pursed her lips, tamping down a look of annoyance. "I'm sorry. I don't know who Sally might have been seen with. Is it important?"

"I'm just looking for clues to Sally's murder."

Eve tucked a stray strand of hair behind her ear, then leaned forward slightly and met my eyes. "I heard some old broad who was having a tantrum over a cake is the one who ended things for Sally. Several of my customers told me she was in custody. Talk about crazy. Who would kill someone over a cake? It makes no sense. Of course, a couple of people told me the woman was on some pretty powerful drugs when she confronted Sally."

"Drugs?"

Eve nodded. "Henrietta from over at the flower shop told me the psycho was in her shop not long before she went to see Sally. She was asking about pink roses, which Henrietta didn't have in stock. Henri said the woman was really loud and overly animated. She thought it was odd, and then she noticed her pupils were dilated and her cheeks flushed. Henri managed to get the woman out the door with a promise to order the roses and have them delivered before the weekend. She had no intention of actually ordering the flowers. She just knew it was best not to confront someone who was so strung out."

I was pretty sure anyone who was close to me knew my least favorite color was pink. It totally fit that Cody's mom would be trying to order flowers I'd hate. Of course, we didn't know each other all that well, so she probably wasn't aware of my aversion to everything pink. She did, however, know we were having a black and white wedding and that the flowers had already been ordered because I'd told her that when she'd asked. But getting worked up over flowers wasn't going to help the situation, so I asked if anyone else had been around who might have witnessed Mrs. West's strange behavior.

"Why don't you ask Henrietta? She should be open today even if it's pouring."

I thanked Eve, took out my umbrella, and headed to the flower shop. The last thing I thought I'd be doing two days before my wedding was wandering around in a storm, looking for proof that the woman who most likely had killed the bakery shop owner actually hadn't.

I paused after I slipped into my car. "I need you to wait here," I said to Cosmo. "I shouldn't be long."

The cat began to purr. I gave him a hug and he settled down on the front seat. The rain was coming down a lot harder now. I was going to be soaked to the skin by the time I got home. Oh well, it couldn't be helped. I really needed my answers.

"Morning, Henrietta," I greeted her after once again shaking the rain from my umbrella, then stashing it in my waterproof sleeve.

"Morning, Cait. Your black and white roses are being delivered tomorrow, although I'm not sure where to send them. Sorry about the church. When we spoke before, you were so excited about getting married there."

"Cody and I have decided to postpone the wedding until we find out when the church will reopen. I was going to talk to you about the flowers. If it isn't too late to cancel them, I'd like to do that. If it's too late to cancel, of course I'll pay for any flowers you have."

"I can probably resell the white roses. The black ones, maybe not. But I'll try. I'll let you know how it works out. I'm really hoping the church will reopen soon. Someone told me it might be closed well into December, which would be tragic for my business. The church orders a lot of flowers from me. When you take into account the flowers for the services and for weddings and funerals, you're talking about a large percentage of my income."

"I guess I hadn't thought of that."

"Most people don't. They figure the church is insured, so being closed for a few weeks is no big deal, but for the small businesses who service it, it's huge."

"I'm so sorry. If it helps, Father Bartholomew told me that he hopes to open the Sunday after Thanksgiving."

Henrietta raised an imaginary glass. "Here's hoping. If the church is closed into December, I'm not sure what I'm going to do."

Suddenly, I felt awful about all the whining I'd been doing. I hadn't stopped to consider how it might affect others in the community. "Listen," I said, "the main reason I came in is to ask about the woman who came in here to order pink flowers on Monday."

Henrietta rolled her eyes. "She was totally high. I mean out-of-her-head-crazy high. I heard she's a suspect in Sally's murder. I guess I should be glad I decided to play along with her instead of arguing with her the way Sally did."

"You're sure she was on drugs?"

"Totally. Not a lot of people know this, but I used to be an emergency room nurse. I treated a lot of strung-out people, so I know one when I see one."

I raised a brow. "You were a nurse? Really? I had no idea. Why did you give up nursing in favor of selling flowers?"

"Generally, selling flowers is a lot less stressful. I woke up one day and realized that while I was only thirty, I had high blood pressure and an ulcer. I knew I needed to make a change if I didn't want to worry myself into an early grave, so I quit my job, moved to Madrona Island, and opened a flower shop. I haven't regretted my decision once."

I picked up a pumpkin-scented candle and gave it a sniff. "I don't suppose you know what type of drug the woman was on?"

"I don't know for certain, but if I had to guess, I'd say some sort of amphetamine, or possibly an antidepressant. It's hard to know without a toxicology screen because people respond differently to drugs."

I wondered if Cody's mom had been given a tox screen. No one had mentioned it to me, so probably not; she hadn't actually been arrested. Still, if she'd been on something, it might explain quite a lot. "So, you're saying someone could have a reaction to drugs that could make them act in a violent and irrational manner, even if what they were taking was legally prescribed?" I clarified.

"Sure. If the drug was new to them and they weren't used to it, or if they took too much of a prescribed drug for some reason, or if they mixed two different drugs that shouldn't have been taken at the same time. Not everyone who came into the ER all strung out was high on illegal drugs. In fact, more often than not, the people we treated had been prescribed the drugs they took."

"Wouldn't the doctor who prescribed the drug know which drugs might interact negatively?"

"Sure, if the same doctor prescribed both drugs. A lot of people go to different doctors for different reasons. Not everyone takes the time to inform their doctors of all the drugs they're already taking."

That made sense. I knew people who saw specialists for different problems. "Was anyone with the woman when she was here?"

"No, she was alone. She seemed to be on foot, which was good, because she was in no condition to drive. She mentioned that she was meeting someone, but she didn't say who or where."

Okay, so who was Mrs. West planning to meet and had she ever done so? I smiled at Henrietta. "Thank you so much for the information. You've definitely given me something to think about."

"I'm happy to help."

I started to leave, then turned around. "You don't know someone named Beth Bennington, do you?"

"Sure, I know Beth."

"I hoped to speak to her about something I heard earlier. Do you know where I can find her?"

"She works in Harthaven, at that little pet shop near the park."

"Thanks. And let me know how much I owe you for the flowers."

"I will, and please let me know if you hear about the church reopening. You'd think the church secretary would call me, but I had to find out about the fire from a customer after I'd already done all the arrangements. I like Father Bartholomew, but things haven't been as organized over there since Father Kilian left. I get that everyone wants to retire at some point, but I really miss him."

"I think he misses everyone too. I'll call you if I hear about the reopening, and thanks again for everything."

Chapter 6

I took out my umbrella and ventured back out into the storm. I still needed to speak to Connie Salisman and Beth Bennington, but first I wanted to see Cody. The idea that his mother might have been under the influence of either a legal or an illegal drug intrigued me. Henrietta had mentioned antidepressants. Could Mrs. West have been having a reaction to a prescription? It seemed worth our while to find out.

I wasn't sure why Cosmo had shown up on the doorstep of the Driftwood Café, but I was sure he probably didn't want to run all over town with me, so I took him back to the cabin, made sure that both he and Max had plenty of food and water, then went back out into the storm. When I arrived at the newspaper office, the door was locked and the interior dark. I texted Cody, who informed me that he was meeting with one of his advertisers but would be back in an hour. I wanted to speak to him as soon as possible, so I told him I was going over to O'Malley's, the bar my brothers owned, to have lunch while I waited. There were some who thought Aiden and Danny should have renamed the bar Hart's because they'd completely remodeled the place, but they felt O'Malley's was an institution on Madrona Island, and it was their intention to keep the O'Malley family and their contribution to the community alive.

"I didn't expect to see you in here at all this week," said Stacy Barnwell, a single mom with two-year-old twins who worked the lunch shift at the bar.

I sat down at a small table for two in front of the crackling fire. "I'm waiting for Cody to get out of a meeting and thought I'd grab some lunch."

"The soup of the day is broccoli cheese, the sandwich is a hot Reuben or grilled cheese, and the burger is either the classic or the black and blue. We also have chicken wings and chili fries."

Due to limited assistance in the kitchen, Danny and Aiden had decided on a limited lunch menu, at least for the winter. They hoped to have full-time help in the kitchen by the time the summer tourist season rolled around. "I'll have the soup with some garlic bread. Are my brothers around?"

"Aiden's working the late shift, but Danny is here somewhere. He was talking to Conway Hilderbrant about the annual football game between O'Malley's and Shots, so they may have gone into the office."

I took off my wet jacket and hung it over a chair to dry. "I was wondering if they were going to do that this year."

"Danny wants to, if they can get enough players. Danny and Aiden are both in, but Libby is pregnant and I tweaked my back, so we're both out. Danny said something about recruiting family. Haven't Cody and Finn played in the past?"

"They have, and I played two years ago and would love to jump into the fray. Are they doing it on Friday again?"

"I'm not sure. I heard something about moving it to Thursday morning because both bars are closed then. Danny said something about a dinner he'd agreed to help out with, so I'm not sure what was decided."

"The dinner is the one Cody and I are giving at Mr. Parsons's house, but that isn't until the evening. His neighbor, Francine Rivers, has taken charge of the cooking, though I probably should be around to help out. Still, I don't suppose she'd mind if Cody and I took a couple of hours off in the morning to help O'Malley's decimate Shots."

"I'm sure the guys would welcome the help. Talk to Danny about it. I'm going to run to get your soup."

The flag football game consisted of eight players on the field at any one time. Each team tried for eleven or twelve players in all, so they had subs to give their starters a break. I suspected the Hart family alone could fill a lot of those spots. Danny, Aiden, Finn, and Cody would all want to play, and so would Cassie. I wasn't sure about Siobhan. In the past, she'd served as a scorekeeper, which was a role I assumed she'd be willing to take on again. Tara wasn't all that athletic, but I figured she would help out with the yardage chains with the bookstore closed on Thanksgiving, and she planned to spend the day with us anyway.

"Hey, Cait. What are you doing here?" Danny asked when he entered the bar.

"I came for soup. I hear you're going to do the flag football game against Shot's next week."

"If we can get enough players."

"I'm in. Cody too. Are you doing it on Thursday?"

"That's what we thought. But you have that huge dinner to get ready for, and I agreed to help."

"The dinner isn't until six, and Francine is handling the food. If you have the game in the morning, say around ten, that should work. It never takes more than a couple of hours. I bet Finn would want to play. I'm not sure about Siobhan, but she might be willing to keep score."

"Actually, Siobhan told me she wanted to play if we had the game at a time that would work for her. Mom's agreed to sit on the sidelines with Connor, and Maggie and Michael committed to keeping score."

"Sounds like a family event. I'm sure Cassie will want to play. Let's do it."

"Are you sure? It seems like your entire cooking squad will be at the park."

"I'll check with Francine. All the volunteers who have agreed to cook a turkey plan to do it on Wednesday. The pies and rolls, as well as most of the sides, will be made ahead of time as well. We've tried to plan it so all we have to do on Thursday is reheat."

"Okay. If you think it will work, we'll go for it. With the family we'd have twelve players, which should be plenty to ensure that O'Malley's takes home the victory mug this year."

I called Francine right away, just to make sure everyone being gone Thursday morning wouldn't send her into a panic. She assured me she had things well under control and that Wednesday was going to be the day she needed all her helpers. Cody and I would be around all day on Wednesday to set up tables and chairs, and to make sure the ballroom was cleaned and decorated for the dinner the following day.

Stacy had just delivered my soup and bread, along with a cup of coffee, when Chappy Longwood walked in. Chappy was an old, weathered fishing captain who'd worked the waters surrounding Madrona Island since before my brothers were born. He'd been a regular at O'Malley's since there'd been an O'Malley's, and my brothers gave him lunch every day on the house.

"Afternoon, Chappy," I said as he saddled up to the bar.

"Afternoon, Cait. Seems like a stormy day to be out and about."

"Last-minute wedding errands," I settled on, even though that wasn't really what I'd been doing at all.

"Do you want the regular?" Stacy asked, after setting a large mug of coffee in front of Chappy.

"As always."

Chappy had a classic burger with a side of French fries every day he had lunch with them. It seemed to me that eating the exact same thing every day would get boring, but I supposed for those who sought stability in their lives, eating the same thing day in and day out would provide just that.

"Don't forget, we'll be closed on Thursday as well as Sunday next week," Stacy reminded him.

"I remember," Chappy grumbled.

"If you don't have plans on Thanksgiving, Cody and I are throwing a feast at Mr. Parsons's place," I said to the white-haired man as he sipped his coffee.

"You gonna have yams?"

"We are," I confirmed.

"With little marshmallows?"

I lifted a shoulder. "Sure, if that's what you like."

"My mama used to make yams with little marshmallows when I was a kid. Sure would love to have some again before I die. What time?"

"Dinner is at six, but I imagine folks will start showing up at around five. Dress is casual and you don't have to bring anything."

"Sounds right nice. Thank you. I'd like to come."

"The kids and I will be there as well," Stacy said. "I can give you a ride if you want."

Chappy smiled, showing off the wide space where his two top front teeth had once been. "That would be very convenient. I still have my old Chevy, but I don't like to drive after dark."

"Okay, then, it's a date," Stacy said. "The kids and I will be by your place at around five."

One of the things I loved most about living on Madrona Island was that the locals, at least the longtime ones, were like a big family. We cared about and looked out for one another. Being part of the Madrona Island family meant that no matter where life took you, you never had to be alone.

After I finished lunch, I headed back to the newspaper. Cody had texted to let me know he was back. I hated how tired and defeated he looked.

"Rough morning?" I asked.

Cody pulled me into his arms and hugged me tight. "I guess you could say that."

"Were you able to talk to your mother?"

He nodded. "She admitted to going to the bakery, but she said she didn't stay long. I asked her where she went after that, because I figured if we could place her somewhere other than Sally's before the last charge at three fifty-five, that would provide an alibi of sorts. She didn't remember. She said she was worked up, so she just walked around a bit. I tried to get her to narrow things down a bit by asking if she'd gone into other shops or which direction she took, but she became more and more agitated the harder I pushed, and eventually, she kicked me out of her room."

"I spoke to Henrietta from the flower shop, who told me your mother was in there just before the bakery. It seems she was asking about pink flowers. Henrietta didn't have any, but she told her she'd order some, just to get her out the door. She used to be a nurse, and she realized your mother was totally strung out."

Cody frowned. "Strung out?"

"Henrietta said she was on drugs. Her pupils were dilated and her cheeks were flushed. She didn't know what sort of drugs she'd taken, but she suspected amphetamines or antidepressants. Do you know if your mom is taking prescribed drugs that might lead to agitation and violent tendencies?"

"I'm really not sure," Cody said. "I know she takes blood pressure medication, and she's taken sleeping pills from time to time. To be honest, I haven't been around her enough recently to know if she's taking any new medication. I'll find out."

"Henrietta used to be an ER nurse, and she mentioned that a lot of folks who came in where she worked strung out on drugs, were taking prescribed drugs they'd had a bad reaction to. She also said drug interactions could play a role if a person was prescribed drugs that didn't work well together."

"Wouldn't a doctor know that?" Cody asked.

"Yes, if the same doctor prescribed both drugs."

"Okay. I'll go back to the inn to ask her about drugs. If she doesn't agree to talk about it, I'll see if I can find her purse and take a look for myself. Did you find out anything else?"

"That Sally might have been having an affair. I don't have all the details, or even proof of the affair, other than someone who claimed to have seen Sally and a man having dinner together and appearing to be intimate. Sally's husband has been away from home a lot between work and caring for his sick mother. An affair is as good a motive for murder as any."

"Is the husband back in town?" Cody asked.

"I don't know. He was in Virginia when Finn called him about Sally's death. It's possible the mystery man is the killer, though the affair might not turn out to mean anything. I think it's worth looking in to."

"Agreed. Anything else?"

"No. I'm going to try to speak to Connie Salisman after I leave here. At this point, I figure the more people I talk to, the greater the odds we'll stumble onto the clue we need."

"I asked my mom about the blood on her clothes," Cody said. "She looked confused, then made a comment about perhaps dripping ketchup on her clothes, but she couldn't remember when that could have been. When I asked her if she wanted me to have her clothes cleaned, she said Eric had taken care of it."

"So she knew Eric had taken away her clothing."

Cody pursed his lips. "Apparently." He looked into my eyes. "I'm really afraid she might be guilty, and I have no idea what I'm going to do if she is."

I put my arms around Cody's waist. "Whatever happens, we'll deal with it together."

******

I left the newspaper to try to track down Connie Salisman. I wasn't holding out a lot of hope she could help me, but she was the last name on my list of people to talk to today, and I wanted to go into tonight's meeting able to discuss everything I'd been assigned to do.

Connie worked as a sorter for the island's only post office. She was usually in the back, processing the mail as it came in, but today I found her at the front counter.

"I don't usually see you up here," I greeted her.

"George wasn't able to make it over from Orcas Island today because of the storm, so I'm the only one here. Today's mail never did make it over from the main sorting center in Seattle, so I've been covering the desk."

"I wasn't aware the ferries weren't running today."

"I guess with the storm it probably wasn't safe to run them."

"There's a lot of wind with this one," I agreed.

"We had a gust off the marina a while ago that I thought was going to shake this building clear off its foundation." Connie glanced out the window. The wind had picked up quite a bit. "Did you come for your mail?"

"Actually, I came to talk to you. I guess you heard about Sally."

"I did, and I still can't believe it. Sally had her moments and could certainly be opinionated and even pushy at times, but she had a good heart. This should never have happened to her."

"I'm asking people who knew her if they have any idea who might have wanted her dead."

"I figured you were working with Finn when you said you wanted to talk about Sally. The truth is, I don't know who would go so far as to kill her. She'd been in a conflict of sorts with Eli Alderman, who mentioned it when he dropped by to mail out the flyers for the chamber mixer. But he's a good guy. He wouldn't hurt anyone."

"I understand Sally was leading a drive to create a second chamber of commerce that would most likely have resulted in Eli losing his job."

Connie nodded. "That's right. And Eli was angry about it. He admitted as much to me. But he said Sally was unlikely to be successful. He was certain most of the business owners on the island were happy with the way things were and wouldn't want to rock the boat."

I jumped as a tree limb hit the side of the building. If the rain kept up throughout the afternoon, the road leading out to the peninsula was bound to flood during high tide. It was time for me to get home. "I understand you and some of the others from exercise class had plans to have dinner with Sally the night she died."

"That's right."

"Did Sally call or text or notify you in any manner that she needed to cancel?"

Connie shook her head. "She didn't call me, but she got in touch with Eve to let her know."

Funny that Eve hadn't brought that up when I spoke to her. "Do you have any idea what time Sally called Eve?"

Connie shook her head. "She didn't say. At the time, none of us knew Sally was dead, so it didn't seem important."

"No, I guess not. I understand there was a rumor that Sally might have been having an affair."

Connie shrugged. "I've heard that, but you know how it is with rumors. Most don't have much truth to them once you dig around a bit. Sally's been involved in the community theater for a while, and it's true there's a new man in that group. I don't know his name or anything about him, but I've heard he's very good-looking. I suppose with her husband away so much, Sally could have let her eye wander."

"So when Sally didn't show up on Monday night, was it just you, Eve, and Connie who met for dinner?"

"And Darla."

"Darla? No one's mentioned her to me before."

"Darla Smith was the one who suggested we all have dinner on Monday. She said she had a business proposition she wanted to present to us."

"A business proposition?"

"She wants to open a Pilates studio and is looking for investors. She attends the same exercise class the rest of us do and hoped we might be interested in a lower-impact form of staying in shape."

A Pilates studio might do well on the island. "Did you decide to invest?"

"No. I don't have the money to do something like that. None of us do, with the exception of Sally. Eve and I talked about it and decided Sally was actually

Darla's target, but she didn't want to be quite that obvious, so she invited the rest of us as filler."

Sally had an accountant husband and owned her own business. It was reasonable to think she might have extra cash to invest. But the others? Not so much.

After I spoke to Connie, I headed out into the storm once again. The rain was coming down even harder than it had been, but I wanted to try to speak to Beth before I went home, so I made a left turn and drove toward Harthaven. I'd never been formally introduced to her, but after I heard where she worked, I realized we'd come into contact when she had a cat she couldn't place and wondered if we'd take him at the Harthaven Cat Sanctuary, which, at the time, had been owned and operated by my Aunt Maggie.

The rain had sent most locals running for cover, so the main street near the marina, which was usually packed with people walking between the shops was all but deserted. I pulled up in front of the pet store and parked on the street. The rain was coming down in sheets with the wind blowing, so I pulled my hood up over my hair and made a run for it.

"It's really coming down out there," Beth said after I jogged in through the front door and shook the moisture from my jacket.

I had to laugh at the absurdity of even being out in this mess. "Yeah, it really is. It's really time for me to head home once I'm done here. I'm surprised you're still open."

"I was just about to lock up. Can I help you?"

"I wanted to ask you about Sally Enderling. I understand you saw her with a man who probably wasn't her husband in a restaurant not long ago."

Beth grinned. "Oh yeah, I saw them. And the guy was a babe. There was no doubt in my mind that Sally was getting some on the side. Not that I blamed her. Her old man was never around."

"Do you happen to know the name of the man you saw Sally with?"

"Hugo. Sally said his name was Hugo when I asked her. He'd recently joined the community theater group Sally belonged to. She said they were just friends, but they sure looked like more than that when I ran into them. Heck, they were holding hands across the table."

"Does Hugo have a last name?" I asked.

"I'm sure he does, but I don't know it. You aren't thinking Sally's Italian lover offed her?"

"Not necessarily. I was just curious about him."

"Sorry I don't have any more information. You ought to check with some of the other members of the theater group. Sue Boatnick is producing the Christmas play. If Hugo is involved, she would know his name."

Chapter 7

Later that evening, everyone gathered in my cabin to go over the status of the investigation. The storm was still raging outside, so Tara had picked up her cat, Bandit, and arranged to spend the night with the others in the main house. She was the only one at the meeting who didn't live on the estate, and it made sense for her to stay.

"Before we begin, I have something to say," Cody began. "As much as I hate to even consider that my mother could have done what she's suspected of, several people have suggested she was acting strangely on the day Sally was killed. I went to see her today, and I have to admit her behavior could only be described as agitated and irrational. I'd spoken to Cait earlier, and she'd spoken to someone who used to be a nurse. This woman told Cait that on the day Sally died, it appeared to her my mother was strung out on drugs. I've never known her to take anything illegal, but I do know she takes several prescription drugs, including a blood pressure medication and sleeping pills. I asked if she'd changed any of her prescriptions or added a new medication recently, and initially, she denied it. We spoke for a while, and she finally admitted she'd been anxious about the wedding, so when my cousin Eric offered her some of his antidepressants, she accepted them. I suspected they interacted with one of her other meds in a negative way, so I took her to the ER. The hospital is keeping her overnight for observation, but the doctor I spoke to said a drug interaction could very well lead to agitation and aggression."

Cody paused, but no one spoke. I didn't think any of us knew what to say. Was Cody throwing in the towel? Was he convinced his mother was guilty of killing Sally?

"What are you saying?" Finn finally asked.

"I don't know. I really hope my mother is innocent, but things seem to be stacking up against her. She's confused about what occurred on Monday afternoon. When I asked her about it, she said she wandered around after she left the bakery. She didn't remember where she was or what she'd been doing. Cait's putting a lot of time into this, and I wanted to be up front about what I'd learned. I know you're all on my side. On my mother's side. But I also know that the truth can end up in a different place than we'd hope."

"I appreciate you being up front with us," Finn said, "and I'm not sure how this investigation will turn out. Sheriff Fowler is fairly convinced your mother is guilty, but he hasn't made an arrest yet, so in my mind that indicates he doesn't have enough evidence to do it, or he has other viable suspects. I think the best use of our time this evening is to discuss those other suspects. Just in case."

"I agree," Siobhan spoke up. "I have something new, and so does Cait. Let's present it to the group." Siobhan looked at Cody. "I can't imagine how hard this must be for you, but I think it would be a mistake to give up now."

"Okay," Cody said. "I'm prepared to go on if the rest of you are."

"Let's go over the suspects to see who should remain on the list, who should be eliminated, and who, if anyone, should be added," Siobhan suggested. She pulled the cap from her dry erase marker. "First, we have Miranda Wells, owner of the trinket shop Sally threatened to put out of business by taking over her lease. I spoke to Miranda today, and she admitted to being angry about the lease. She'd been in negotiations with the owner of the building and hoped she would be able to remain as a tenant. I sensed her irritation, but I didn't pick up on anything that would suggest aggression to the point of murder. If you remember, Miranda told Cassie she'd heard the ruckus in the bakery and went out onto the sidewalk to take a peek. She looked in the window and saw someone, probably Mrs. West, arguing with Sally, but a group from the ferry went into her shop, so she headed back in. Today, Miranda was able to provide sales receipts that seemed to back up the fact that she had customers to deal with during the time we suspect Sally might have died."

"Do we have a better idea of when Sally was killed yet?" I asked Finn.

"As we know, the two witnesses who were passing the bakery saw Sally arguing with Mrs. West at around three thirty, and there's an entry in the register tape for a sale at three fifty-five. We don't know if Mrs. West was still there then, but we have no reason not to believe Sally was the one to record the sale. She usually locked up at four, but Carla found the door unlocked the next morning, so we're operating under the assumption that someone was either already in the shop when four o'clock rolled around or arrived at about that time. It's even possible whoever made the purchase at three fifty-five is the one who kill her."

"Is it possible Sally was distracted and forgot to lock up but was killed later in the afternoon?" Cassie asked.

"Sure, I guess so," Finn answered. "The ME has put the time of death at between three and seven. We've been focusing on a time of death of around four o'clock due to the information we have. But something might have happened to distract Sally to make her forget to lock up at four. After her last customer left, she could have headed into the kitchen to clean up and prepare for the next day's baking, allowing someone to take advantage of the open door, slip in, and kill her."

"Might there be someone else who had a key?" Cassie asked.

"According to Carla, she and Sally, and possibly Sally's husband Nick, who was three thousand miles away in Virginia at the time of Sally's death, are the only ones with keys," Finn said.

"Are we sure Nick Enderling really was in Virginia on Monday?" I asked.

Finn glanced at me. "That's where I was told he was when I first spoke to Carla, and that's where he told me he was when I spoke to him on the phone."

"I've spoken to several people today who've indicated Sally may have been having an affair with a new man on the island, someone she met through her theater group. I don't have any proof of that yet, but if Sally was unfaithful to her husband and he found out about it, that would give him a very good motive for murder."

"I'll talk to him again," Finn said. "I'll see if he has proof of where he was on Monday."

Siobhan highlighted Nick Enderling's name on the suspect list. "Does anyone else stand out?" she asked.

"Has anyone spoken with Eli Alderman?" I asked.

"I know the sheriff has," Finn answered.

"What about Devita Colter?" I asked.

"The sheriff spoke to her as well. She was alone in her bakery getting a head start on cookies and pastries for the following day on Monday, so she doesn't have an alibi. Even without one, the sheriff isn't considering her a strong suspect. I can speak to her personally tomorrow."

We chatted for a while longer, but we didn't have a lot of new information to narrow things down. The subject changed to the upcoming holiday, and once that conversation had been exhausted, we said our good nights and the others made their way to the main house. I suspected that despite our efforts to find an alternate suspect, we were still pretty much convinced Cody's mom was going to end up the one still standing when the others had been eliminated.

I poured two glasses of wine and handed one to Cody. "You know we're going to figure this out."

He let out a long sigh. "I know. I guess I'm kind of afraid of the truth." He set down the wine I'd just handed him. "I'm not very good company tonight. I think I'll go back to my place."

I nodded, though I wanted to cry. "Okay. I understand. Will you call me tomorrow?"

"I'll come by in the morning before I head to the hospital." Cody pulled me into his arms and kissed me. "Thanks for understanding that I need some time to think."

I reached up and kissed him on the cheek. "I'll miss you tonight, but I do understand. I'll see you in the morning."

Cody went out to his truck, and I picked up my wine and drank it down in one gulp. Up until a couple of days ago, I'd expected to be married on Saturday. The way things were going now, I wondered if the wedding I'd been putting off for so long, then finally committed to, was going to happen after all. I pulled both Max and Cosmo into my arms and wept until I had no more tears to shed.

Chapter 8

Friday, November 16

I'd barely slept a wink the night before, as I tossed and turned and fretted about the situation and where it might lead. I hated seeing Cody so upset. It wasn't at all like him to choose to spend time away from me when he knew Mr. Parsons was taken care of, so I was happy and relieved when he showed up at my cabin the next morning with a huge smile on his face.

"You look happy," I said with a feeling of hope tinged with uncertainty.

Cody pulled me into his arms and gave me a lingering kiss. "I am. Finn called me early this morning to tell me the sheriff had made an arrest."

"I assume based on your smile that the person arrested was someone other than your mother?"

Cody nodded. "Sheriff Fowler received an anonymous tip from 'a concerned citizen' yesterday afternoon, saying they'd seen Miranda Wells leaving the bakery at around four fifteen, after it should have been closed for the day. The witness said Miranda seemed sort of spooked and was looking around a lot as she exited the shop. Based on the tip, the sheriff was able to obtain a warrant to search Miranda's shop and home and found a rolling pin with blood on it hidden in the storage room of the store."

Talk about something being just a tad too convenient. "Did the blood belong to Sally?"

"It's being tested, but it seems obvious what happened. Sally was threatening to put Miranda out of business by taking over the space she leases for her trinket shop. The suspicion from the beginning has been that Sally was hit over the head with a rolling pin, or something shaped like it, and a rolling pin with blood on it was found in Miranda's storage room. Seems open and shut to me."

I was less convinced this mess was really over, but he looked so happy that I forced a smile to my face. "I'm so relieved this seems to be cleared up. How's your mother?"

"She's obviously happy she's off the hook. I spoke to the doctor in the hospital, and he said she should be fine. She's been instructed not to take anything but her blood pressure medication until her doctor in Florida is able to do a full workup."

"So she's going home?"

Cody nodded. "We discussed it and decided that would be best. We aren't sure when the wedding is going to take place, and Mom and Eric can't stay here indefinitely. Mom already has an appointment with her doctor next week, so I booked them on a flight out of Seattle tomorrow morning at six a.m. I'll take them over on the ferry today and spend the night in Seattle with them. I should be home by midafternoon."

"That sounds like a good plan." I hugged Cody. "I'm so happy things worked out."

Cody ran a hand through his hair. "Me too. I have to say, I was really sweating bullets for a while. I hated thinking my own mother was guilty of taking another person's life, but the way things were stacking up, I couldn't help but consider the possibility."

"I know how hard this has been on you." I hugged Cody again, wished him a safe trip, and sent him on his way. Then I looked at Cosmo. "This isn't over, is it?"

"Meow."

"Yeah, it seems too convenient to me too. I'm glad Sheriff Fowler isn't focusing on Mrs. West anymore, but Miranda as the killer doesn't work for me."

"Meow." The cat began to wind through my legs.

"There are too many loose ends and unanswered questions."

"Meow."

"For one thing, if someone saw Miranda come out of Sally's bakery on Monday afternoon, why did they wait all this time to make the anonymous call? Her body was found on Tuesday. Why would anyone wait until Thursday to tell what they knew?"

"Meow."

I picked up the cat and cuddled him to my chest. "The rain has let up a bit, although I understand there's more on the way. I'm going to take Max for a quick run while it's still dry out. When I get back, I'll work on this some more. I don't want to do anything that might cast doubt on Mrs. West again, but if Miranda is innocent, I don't want her to go to jail."

I bundled up against the cold and Max and I headed out. The sky was still dark and the beach wet, but the wind had died down and the rain had ceased, at least temporarily. Max was happy to be outside no matter the chill in the air. He showed his joy by running up and down the beach chasing seagulls. I didn't blame him for having so much energy after being cooped up inside for the better part of two days. The island depended on regular rain for its water supply, but long days of rain without end had both of us feeling antsy.

Of course, unlike Max, I'd had plenty to occupy my mind and time during the storm. The stressful week had left me and Cody miserable, and everything was still so up in the air. Although I wasn't at all comfortable with the way things had ended up, the anonymous caller had done us a huge favor. Cody was happy. Mrs. West was on her way home, which made me happy. I had a wedding to try to get back on track, and it certainly wasn't my responsibility to find the real killer if Miranda was innocent. I was sure she'd hire a competent attorney who would help her out. Wouldn't it be best for everyone if I let it go?

"Damn." I picked up a long stick and tossed it for Max. As much as I wanted to, my conscience wouldn't let me turn a blind eye when a woman I was pretty sure was innocent might be locked up for a murder she didn't commit. Hopefully, if Miranda *was* innocent, we'd find the real killer, and all roads wouldn't lead back to Mrs. West.

When Max and I returned to the cabin I decided to call Finn before I did anything else. He, like me, had

Cody's best interests at heart, and both of us would want to see that the right person did time for Sally's death.

He picked up on the first ring.

"Where are you?" I asked. "I can hear waves crashing in the background."

"I'm at the old lighthouse on the east shore, interviewing witnesses from the fire."

"The lighthouse? There was a fire? I hadn't heard."

"A small fire that fortunately was caught early on. The damage was minimal, but the lighthouse will be closed indefinitely. The building is old and its structural integrity will have to be looked at very closely before it reopens. I imagine you've spoke to Cody."

"Yes. And while I'm extremely relieved Mrs. West has been allowed to leave the island, I'm still concerned."

"You don't think Miranda Wells is guilty."

I sighed. "I have no idea. She seemed to have motive, and she was right next door. She could easily have snuck over to the bakery at almost any point. It isn't that I necessarily think she's innocent; it's more that I find the anonymous tip and the rolling pin suspect."

Finn groaned. "Yeah, me too. I was shocked when the sheriff arrested Miranda before he was able to obtain the lab reports on the rolling pin, which did seem to turn up conveniently."

"Were Miranda's fingerprints on it?"

"No. There weren't any prints at all, which seems odd. It could be it was fresh out of the dishwasher, and the killer might have been wearing gloves."

"No. Hitting someone over the head with something close at hand is a crime of passion. Wearing gloves to carry out a crime would be premeditated. It feels like Miranda is being set up."

"That's what she's claiming," Finn informed me. "She's insisted from the beginning that she was alone in her store until around four, when a group of tourists came in and made some purchases. They paid cash, and because they were out-of-towners, they're likely long gone from the island. She has sales receipts to back up her story, but they could have been faked, and without names and contact information to go with them, she doesn't really have an alibi at all. She's adamant that she's innocent and has no idea where the rolling pin came from, though she's certain it was planted."

"I have a feeling she's right. I think she *is* being set up. I have to ask myself, why did this anonymous witness wait so long to come forward? Most of the locals knew Sally had been murdered on Tuesday, and anyone who didn't would more than likely have seen the article in Wednesday's newspaper. Why wait until Thursday to call it in?"

"Good question. I find the fact that she didn't think to dispose of the rolling pin hard to understand. A guilty person would have been stupid to keep the murder weapon."

"Exactly. I'm glad Mrs. West is off the hook, and more relieved than I can express that she and Eric are on their way back to Florida, but I can't let go of this yet."

"There's something odd going on. The sheriff was really intent on finding Sally's killer, which I understand, especially given their relationship. That makes it even stranger that he was willing to accept the anonymous tip so easily."

"Is it possible the sheriff knows something about Miranda we don't? Something that would convince him the evidence he found was real and not planted?"

"Perhaps," Finn admitted. "I gotta go. The fire marshal's here. I'll call you later and we can compare notes."

I made a sandwich, then sat down at my dining table to eat it. I'd grabbed a notepad and pen in the event inspiration struck, but so far all I'd accomplished was a fairly intricate doodle. If Miranda hadn't killed Sally, who had? And why out of all the possible suspects had the real killer decided to set Miranda up? It would have been easier to pin the murder on Mrs. West. Pretty much everyone already thought she'd done it anyway. I'd suspect her of making the anonymous call to get herself off the hook, but she'd been in the hospital when it came in. Maybe Eric? I should have asked Finn if the caller was male or female. I couldn't resist calling him back.

"I know you're busy, but I just have one quick question: Was the anonymous call made by a male or a female?"

"The voice was muffled and obviously disguised, but the sheriff thought the call was made by a woman."

"And there's no record of the number used to make the call?"

"Actually, it was traced to the business line at the Driftwood Café."

I frowned. "That's a public place. Wasn't anyone able to figure out who made the call?"

"The sheriff interviewed every staff person on duty Thursday afternoon, and no one admitted to making the call or knowing who did. Someone could be lying, but the manager told the sheriff the office is in a hallway that also leads to the bathrooms. The office door is usually kept closed, but it isn't always locked. It would be possible for a customer to sneak in and make the call without anyone noticing if they were familiar with the layout of the restaurant and knew the phone was there."

"What time did the call come in?" I asked.

"Around three o'clock."

"So the restaurant would be fairly deserted. Not only was it raining hard yesterday, but three o'clock is between lunch and dinner. It should be easy to get a list of all the customers who were there at three o'clock."

"Good point. I imagine the sheriff's already thought of that, but we haven't had a chance to speak much because he's on San Juan Island today, and I've been stuck up here on the east shore all morning."

I bit my lower lip, a habit I seemed to have developed during the stress of the past couple of weeks. "I'll go by the café to chat with Kimmy. I was there to speak to Eve earlier in the day yesterday, so I know she was working the reception desk. I bet either Eve or Kimmy can tell me who was dining at around that time."

"If you're going to continue to snoop around, be careful. If Miranda isn't guilty, Sally's real killer is still out there."

"Don't worry, I'll be careful."

I grabbed my backpack and jacket. Both Max and Cosmo looked at me with hopeful eyes. If they came with me, they'd just end up waiting in the car, and I said as much to them, but neither appeared to care. Of course, Max most likely had no idea what I was yammering about. I suspected Cosmo understood every word I said, and his desire to accompany me on my errand inclined me to take him. I still intended to have a heart-to-heart with the cat, but maybe his presence today would lead me to the clue I suspected was still to be found.

"Okay, you can both come, but remember, I warned you about having to wait in the car while I visit the café."

Cosmo meowed and Max barked. I looked out the window at the dark sky. I had a feeling the pause in the rain wasn't going to last much longer. According to the weather report, the second band of the storm wasn't due until later this evening, but it looked as if it was going to be early.

I opened the cabin's side door, then headed to my car. Both animals jumped in when I opened the back door. I closed it and climbed into the driver's seat, started the motor, and pulled onto the peninsula drive. I wasn't sure if either Kimmy or Eve would be working today, but the odds were one of them would be on shift and willing to talk about the mysterious caller, who, in my mind, had the potential to either confirm what the sheriff already believed or blow the case wide open.

Chapter 9

The Driftwood was slightly more crowded than it had been yesterday, but not by much. Kimmy was at the front counter, as I hoped. She was with a customer when I arrived, so I indicated that I'd grab a table, then made a motion to let her know I wanted to speak to her when she had a minute.

"Hey, Cait; what can I get you?" the waitress asked.

"Just coffee. I'm waiting to talk to Kimmy. Were you working yesterday?"

"No, I'm just Fridays and Saturdays. I have another full-time job. This is just to supplement it so I can make my rent payments."

"I've heard rents on the island have gone up quite a bit."

"A lot. It won't be long before the people who work here won't be able to afford to live here. I'll go grab that coffee."

By the time I'd drunk half the cup, Kimmy came over to join me. "Hey, Cait. What's up?"

"Sheriff Fowler must have already talked to you about the anonymous call that was made from here yesterday."

"Yeah, he was in. He talked to everyone on shift yesterday. I worked breakfast and lunch, so I got off at two thirty, but I hung around, so he interviewed me too."

"You hung around after you got off?"

"I'd gone into the kitchen to grab something to eat. One of the perks of working here is the free meals you can order either before or after your shift. When I work the early shift I usually eat after."

"Who worked the hostess shift after you?"

"Alice Porter. She was here from two thirty to nine o'clock."

"So you were in the kitchen at three o'clock?"

Kimmy nodded. "Sort of. Right off the kitchen is a small room with a table where staff can eat. If you're wondering if I knew who was here at the time of the call, the sheriff asked me that, and I don't. Other than Alice, me, the cook, and Eve, who worked a double shift because a dinner-shift waitress called to let us know she wasn't going to make it in."

"I didn't see Eve when I came in just now. Is she here?"

Kimmy shook her head. "She's off today. In fact, she won't be in until Monday."

"Was the sheriff able to speak to her?" I asked.

Kimmy wrinkled her brow. "I'm not sure. He might have tried calling her cell. I think she's on San Juan Island visiting her boyfriend on her days off."

"Is the cook who was here yesterday here today?"

"He has the dinner shift today, so he'll be in later. Alice is waiting tables in the back room. Of the staff who were here both yesterday afternoon and right now, she's the most likely to have noticed which customers were in."

I chatted with Kimmy for a few more minutes before she had to get back to work. She promised to send Alice over as soon as she had a minute to take a break. I sipped my coffee while I waited. The café was far from packed, but there was enough business that I knew Alice wouldn't have long to chat. Fortunately for me, she was able to make her way to my table in just a few minutes.

"Hey, Cait. Kimmy said you had some questions for me. I have maybe two minutes before I have to get back to work."

"I'll make it quick. I understand you worked the hostess station yesterday afternoon."

"Yes, that's right."

"Do you remember who was here at around three o'clock?"

"The sheriff asked me the same thing. As far as I can remember, there were six customers and five staff. Herman Vincent was the cook on shift until four, when the dinner crew arrived. Eve Donner was waiting tables, after agreeing to a double shift. Polly Simpson was waiting tables too. She came in late, but I'm pretty sure she was here by three. Kimmy was off but still on the premises. And I was here, of course."

"There weren't any managers working?"

"No, not at that time of day. Technically, Herman is in charge when no one else is around."

"So the business office was deserted?"

Alice nodded. "As far as I know it was, and yes, the door is often left open. I know Eve went in to make a call after she agreed to stay for a second shift, and I'm pretty sure Polly used the phone to check in with her babysitter."

"Why would staff use that phone? Why wouldn't they just use their cells?"

"We aren't allowed to have our cell phones on us while we're on shift. Most of us leave them at home or in our vehicles. There's a place to leave purses and other personal possessions in the office, but most of us just don't bring our things inside with us."

"And your car keys?"

"We leave them in the cash register. We drop them off when we come on duty and pick them up when we leave. I have less than a minute left, so I'll go ahead and tell you what I can anticipate you'll want to know. There were six customers here between about two thirty and three thirty: Francine Rivers was having coffee with Nora Bradley, Carla Hudson was having a late lunch with a man whose name I didn't catch, but I'm pretty he's an attorney from the bits of conversation I overheard, and Eli Alderman was having coffee with Oliver Patton. Now I really gotta go. We're short-staffed today."

I felt a bit shell-shocked by the quick list of customers. Francine and Nora were close friends and often dined together. I had no reason to suspect either of them of any involvement in Sally's death, so I immediately crossed them off my mental list. The fact that Carla had been having lunch with a man who appeared to be an attorney was interesting. They could just be friends, but I'd be interested to learn what they were discussing. I still hadn't found out who'd inherited the bakery from Sally and wondered if she had some sort of contract that would give Carla first option in the event of a sale. She'd been with

Sally since she moved to the island and had been the one doing most of the baking. It seemed to me that she'd served as more than a mere employee and therefore could have had a contract of some sort.

The most interesting customers in my book were Eli Alderman and Oliver Patton. Eli certainly had a lot to gain from Sally's death, and while Oliver claimed not to have heard anything when Sally was killed, I suspected he knew more than he was letting on. It had crossed my mind that Eli had been the one to kill Sally and Oliver knew it, and might be using his knowledge to get something from Eli. Of course, Finn had indicated that the anonymous caller was most likely a woman, so it was unlikely it was either of these men.

I finished my coffee, said goodbye to Kimmy, and headed out to my car. I'd hoped knowing who'd been in the café would help me narrow in on a suspect, but I still didn't have a strong feeling about who might be setting Miranda up, if that was what was going on.

"So, what now?" I asked Max and Cosmo. Neither animal answered in any way, but I felt I needed a minute to think and didn't want to sit in my car in front of the café, so I headed down the street to Coffee Cat Books. Tara, Cassie, and Willow, were all working today. Maybe they could help me work through the information I'd just gathered.

When we arrived at the bookstore, I opened the back door, lifted Cosmo out, and told Max to jump down. With another storm on the horizon, there were very few people out and about, so the three were decorating the shop for the upcoming Christmas season.

"Oh look, it's Cait and the kids." Cassie laughed.

"Cait and the kids are out running errands and decided to stop by," I said, putting Cosmo on the floor. I glanced at the empty cat lounge and then back at Cassie. "You didn't bring in any cats?"

"Tara and I talked about it and decided to give the lounge a really good cleaning. There isn't anyone around to adopt the cats anyway."

"I guess that makes sense. The whole town is dead. I stopped by the Driftwood and they had a few customers, but nowhere near what they'd normally have at this time of day."

"I heard the sheriff arrested Miranda Wells for Sally's murder," Willow said.

"So I've been told." I couldn't help but frown.

"You don't seem as happy and relieved as I expected you to be," Tara said.

"I'm relieved. And I'm very happy Mrs. West is off the hook and on her way home to Florida. It's just that things don't feel right."

"Miranda's arrest did seem sort of sudden," Tara admitted.

"I understand it was brought about by an anonymous witness," Willow joined in.

"And therein lies the problem," I said. "Who is this witness? Are they credible? And what's up with the anonymity?"

"All good questions," Tara said.

"According to Finn, the call was made from a landline at the Driftwood Café. I just went by to speak to some of the people who were on duty at the time the call was made. Alice Porter told me there were only six customers then: Francine Rivers was having coffee with Nora Bradley, Carla Hudson was having lunch with a man Alice believed might have been an attorney from what she overheard of their conversation, and Eli Alderman was having coffee with Oliver Patton. I have no reason to suspect either Francine or Nora, though Finn said the call was most likely made by a female, which seems to eliminate Eli and Oliver, so that just leaves Carla. The thing is, Carla said she went to pick up her daughter at three o'clock. We suspect Sally's time of death was closer to four, so she could have come back, but why would Carla sit on the news that she'd seen Miranda with the rolling pin once she discovered Sally was dead? That makes no sense."

"And Carla's the one who told me about Miranda and the dispute with her lease," Tara reminded me. "If she'd seen Miranda leaving the shop at around the time of death, that would have been the perfect time to bring it up."

"Still, the fact that three of the six customers when the call was made are in one way or another involved in the case seems odd to me," Willow said.

She had a point. Carla had been Sally's employer and had been the one to find her body the morning after she was killed, Oliver owned the business in the shop next door to Sally's bakery, and Eli and Sally had been feuding over the development of a second chamber of commerce.

"It seems like Eli had the most to gain from Sally's death," I said. "His alibi was weak and he seemed to be feeling a lot of rage toward her. The possibility that he killed her and then tried to place the blame on someone easy makes sense, but the sheriff told Finn the caller seemed to be female."

"It's not all that hard for a man to disguise his voice to sound like a female," Cassie said.

"I guess that's true."

"What does the cat think?" Willow asked.

I looked around for Cosmo but didn't see him right away. "I'm not sure. I was going to try to talk with him, but I keep getting distracted and haven't gotten around to it. Did you see where he went?"

"I think he went down the hallway," Cassie said.

I headed down the hallway, where the office, bathroom, and storage room were located. The door to the office was cracked open. I pushed it open all the way to find Cosmo on the desk. When I walked in, he swatted a piece of paper onto the floor. It landed at my feet. I bent over and picked it up.

"This is a list of assignments from Francine to all her cooking helpers for the Thanksgiving dinner," I said.

Tara had followed me to the office. "She dropped it off an hour ago."

I frowned. "Francine was at the café yesterday at the time the call was made. Maybe she saw something."

Willow was behind Tara. "The cats are usually the key," she said. "You should talk to Francine."

I set the list back on the desk. "I will." I turned and headed back to the front of the bookstore.

"With Cody gone tonight, why don't the two of us grab some dinner?"

I smiled. "That sounds nice. Do you want me to meet you somewhere?"

"I'll pick you up. Is six okay?"

"Six is great." I picked up the cat. "I'll see you then."

After I left the bookstore, I dropped both Cosmo and Max off at the cabin and went on foot to

Francine's home, which was just down the beach. The peninsula was divided into three estates: one had been handed down through the Hart family for generations, one was presently owned by Francine, who had inherited it from her father, and the third belonged to Mr. Parsons, who also had inherited the land from his ancestors. The lots grew wider as they moved away from the beach, so the distance by water between the estates wasn't all that far. By car, the distance was greater, with the three properties sharing an access road.

I approached Francine's home from the rear and knocked on the back door. After a minute a light went on and then a lock released. "Cait," Francine said. "I wasn't expecting you today."

"I wasn't sure you were home, but I wanted to talk to you, so I took a chance and stopped by."

"I'm just home to grab a bite to eat and then I'll be going out. Would you like some soup?"

"Thanks, but I've already eaten."

Francine stepped aside to let me in. "Well then, you can watch me eat while we chat. What's on your mind?"

I shook the rain from my umbrella, then followed Francine down the short hallway to her kitchen. "I guess you heard Miranda Wells was arrested for Sally Enderling's murder."

"Siobhan mentioned it when I stopped by to give her a cooking schedule for the party. You and Cody must be so relieved that his mother is no longer a suspect."

"Of course, but I do wonder about the timing of the anonymous tip. Apparently, the call was made from the Driftwood Café at around three o'clock yesterday afternoon. I understand you were there with Nora Bradley at the time."

"We were sharing a piece of the delicious blackberry pie that was one of the Thursday specials while we discussed the garden club Christmas party."

"There are two extensions to the phone line in the café, one at the hostess station and one in the business office. It seems no manager was in yesterday using the office, and someone took that opportunity to use the phone to call in the tip. The office is just down the back hallway to the bathrooms. I was wondering if you saw anyone going down the hallway while you were there."

"I wasn't paying any attention, although I was facing in that direction. I don't remember seeing anyone heading into the hallway. Well, I do remember seeing Eve going into the hallway. She waited on us and just happened to say she needed to call her boyfriend to let him know she was working a double shift because her softball game had been canceled. There weren't a lot of customers at that time of day. I don't recall seeing anyone else."

"I understand Carla Hudson was there."

Francine nodded. "Yes. She was meeting with Sally's attorney."

"Sally's attorney?"

"Sally and Carla were partners, it seems. I believe Sally was the majority owner, and I'm not sure what percentage Carla owns, but Carla moved to the island and gave up the chance to open her own bakery to help Sally, so she gave her a share of the business. I think Carla was meeting the attorney to go over her options now that Sally's gone."

"Did you notice Carla get up and leave her table at any point?" I asked.

"No. But I was focused on my conversation with Nora and wasn't paying attention to the other customers."

The news about Carla's partial ownership in the bakery seemed significant, although I wasn't sure how it fit into the big picture yet. Other than Carla, Francine and Nora were the only female customers when the call was made, and I'd already decided there was no reason to suspect them, which left me struggling to think who could have made the call. Could there have been someone else in the café? Someone who could have made the call and then hidden in the bathroom for a while should someone notice them leaving the hallway? Or maybe it had been Eli and he'd disguised his voice to make it appear the call had been made by a woman?

******

"What's all this?" I asked that evening after I walked into Antonio's with Tara.

"Surprise," shouted Siobhan, Cassie, my mom, Maggie, Willow, Maggie's best friend Marley, and Aiden's sort-of girlfriend, Alanna Quinn.

Tara grinned. "When I made the reservation, you were getting married tomorrow and this was going to be your bachelorette party. In the commotion of the past week, I forgot to cancel it. But when you told me Cody was going to be out of town, I figured why not go ahead with the party anyway?"

I felt myself tear up. "That's so nice of you." I placed a hand on my heart. "All of you."

Tara pulled out a chair. "Have a seat and order a drink. A strong one. We all have something we'd like to say before we order our meals."

To say I was overwhelmed by the toast each person made was putting it mildly, yet somehow I made it through the speeches without crying until my mother started in about the night I was born and Cassie finished things off with a speech about having the best big sister a girl ever had. By the time Tara and I made it back to my cabin, I was a tiny bit tipsy and a bundle of emotions.

I hugged Tara. "Thank you so much. I wasn't sure I wanted to do something like that, but it turned out to be one of the most memorable nights of my life. Now I just hope the wedding will actually happen so the party will be justified."

"The wedding will happen. Maybe not tomorrow, but it will happen."

"I hope so. This week has been really tense for me, and extra-hard on Cody. I'd like next week not to be equally difficult."

"You aren't sure Miranda's the one who killed Sally, and after speaking to you this afternoon, I understand why you have your doubts. But Mrs. West is on her way home, so even if you can prove Miranda is innocent, neither Cody nor his mother will have another week like the last one."

I hoped Tara was right, but somehow I suspected she wasn't.

Chapter 10

Monday, November 19

It had been three days since my bachelorette party and Cody and I were no closer to setting a date for our wedding. Father Bartholomew had called to let me know that the damage in the church rafters was worse than was first realized, so it wouldn't be reopening until mid-December. Cody's mother and cousin were safely tucked away in Florida, which was a good thing because the lab results had revealed that the blood on the rolling pin found in Miranda's store wasn't Sally's. Additionally, Carla had assured the sheriff that the rolling pin used to try to pin Sally's murder on Miranda was a cheap one that could be found in any dollar store and most assuredly wouldn't have been found in Sally's bakery.

I wasn't sure where the sheriff stood in terms of suspects, but Finn had shared that Mrs. West was still on the list of suspects, although they didn't have near enough on her to arrest her or to request her return to the island. Cody had counseled her to stay far away from Madrona Island until after the murder was solved.

Cody was at Mr. Parsons's this morning, clearing out the ballroom for the tables and chairs he'd rented and would be delivered tomorrow. I sat at my kitchen counter sipping a cup of coffee, trying to figure out how things stood with the Scooby murder investigation. It was almost Thanksgiving and I had a wedding to try to resuscitate. I doubted anyone would blame me if I walked away from the whole thing. Of course, Cosmo was still with me, so I supposed the universe still wanted me to be involved. I knew I'd have a tough time enjoying my new life as Cody's wife with an unsolved murder hanging over my head.

I took out a pen and pad of paper and started a list. The first thing I needed to do was to try to assess who was still a suspect and who'd been cleared.

The first name I wrote down was Miranda Wells. Sure, she had already been arrested, and that had turned out to be based on false evidence. What I wondered now was whether the fact that she'd been framed definitively meant she was innocent. All we really knew was that the rolling pin used to frame her was a phony. Did that mean the anonymous tip was phony as well? Did it mean the person who made the call was the killer? If that was so, all we needed to do was to identify that person. But if the call was made by someone other than the killer, was it reasonable to assume Miranda could still be the killer?

I mulled this over for quite a while as I sipped yet another cup of coffee. What was that, four cups? I'd better make this my last or I would be bouncing off the walls. I supposed there could be a case made that

Miranda, who most definitely had motive and opportunity, could have killed Sally, that someone knew it but didn't have the proof they needed so foolishly planted fake evidence, thinking that would be enough. And then there was the charge on the cash register tape at three fifty-five. The person who came in and purchased the cookies hadn't been identified. Was it possible Miranda had rung up the charge to fool people?

Then there was Eli Alderman. Some people seemed to think he was a nice guy who would never hurt a fly, but in my experience, even nice guys could be driven to acts of violence under the right set of circumstances. Sally's planned actions would threaten Eli's job, and he'd met Oliver Patton at the time the anonymous call was made. I decided to keep Eli on my list as well.

Next was Devita Colter. Sure, she was a tiny thing, and it was hard to imagine her having either the height or strength to hit Sally hard enough with a rolling pin to kill her, but she didn't have an alibi and Sally's bakery had hurt her business, so she really should also be left on the list.

Which brought us to Sally's husband. If she'd been having an affair, it would seem he had motive. He was supposed to have been in Virginia at the time of the murder, but I didn't know whether Finn or the sheriff had tracked down any concrete proof of that yet.

I looked up from my list as Siobhan knocked once and walked in through my side door. "Maggie made cinnamon rolls if you're hungry."

"Sounds good, but I already ate. I might come by to snag one later if there are any left."

"What are you working on?" Siobhan sat down across from me.

"A list of suspects in Sally's murder. I know I should just let it go with everything I have going on, but I can't seem to do that."

"I guess I get that." Siobhan cocked her head to the side. "So, who do you have?"

"The person who made the call to frame Miranda Wells, Miranda Wells, Eli Alderman, Devita Colter, the person who made the bakery purchase at three fifty-five, and Nick Enderling." I briefly explained why I had each person on the list.

"Maybe we should see if Finn has any additional information since we spoke as a group. We haven't met since Thursday evening."

"I'm up to getting together this evening." The next few days were going to be hectic, but I wanted to put this mystery to bed.

"Let's meet here. Maggie and Michael don't seem to mind babysitting Connor."

"Great. I'll call Tara to let her know. Cassie is at the bookstore, so she can tell her. Cody should be back as soon as he finishes clearing out the ballroom, so we'll make something for dinner."

Siobhan stood up. "I'm going back. Connor is napping, but he should be awake soon. If you want one of the cinnamon rolls, you might want to come get it before they're all gone."

I looked at my list again after Siobhan left. Then I looked at Cosmo. "What do you think? Did I miss anyone?"

"Meow."

I considered the clues the cat had given me so far. There'd only been two: the pages in the newspaper and the visit to Francine. With both of them, as with every clue I received from every cat I'd worked with, there was always a doubt in my mind about whether I was interpreting things correctly.

I wasn't certain what information Francine had given me that might turn out to be relevant. She'd been at the café when the anonymous tip was called in to the sheriff, but she hadn't seen anything that pointed me in a particular direction. I'd saved the newspaper the cat had led me to. Had the passage of time allowed me to look at those two pages in a different way?

I considered the ad for the upcoming Christmas Festival and didn't see how it could mean anything. I noted the article in the series Cody had been writing about the history of land acquisition on the island to current times and found that to be unrelated as well. There was the article about the old church that had burned to the ground at the hands of an arsonist, which reminded me that there had been fires in three of our older buildings recently. I doubted the fires were connected to Sally's murder, though I did wonder if they were related to one another.

Then there was the ad for Black Friday deals. The merchants listed were Trinkets and Treasures, Ship Wreck Art and Novelties, Herbalities, Bait and Stitch, Madrona Island Gifts, and Coffee Cat Books.

Under the Community Announcements banner was the paragraph about St. Patrick's, a reminder that the chamber of commerce wouldn't be meeting this week, a call for actors for the annual Christmas play, and a mention that the annual Thanksgiving food drive was today. The only other items were ads for Sally's bakery and Madrona Island Baked Goods.

I'd never followed up with Sue Boatnick about the new actor in the community theater and his possible relationship with Sally. I also hadn't spoken personally to Devita. I'd known her since I was a little girl and she'd always seemed like a nice woman. I couldn't imagine her being a killer, but if I wanted to solve this case, and I did, I needed to follow all the leads that presented themselves.

Making a quick decision, I chose to head to Madrona Island Baked Goods to talk to Devita. I bundled up against the damp air and took my car to Harthaven.

"Morning, Devita," I said to the woman who'd been baking and serving customers since before I was born.

"Been a while since you've been in."

I cringed. I felt bad about that. Devita's pastries were very good, but Sally's were better. "I don't come into Harthaven as often now that we've opened the bookstore in Pelican Bay. I'd love a chocolate doughnut today."

Devita set a doughnut on a napkin, then slid it onto the counter. "Coffee?"

"Sure. Seems like a coffee kind of day."

I paid Devita but lingered. I wasn't sure how to bring up the reason I was there. "I guess you heard about Sally."

Devita nodded. "I did."

Okay, Cait, you're going to need to do better than that if you want to get a conversation going. "I heard they arrested Miranda Wells but let her go when they found out the blood on the rolling pin that was found in her store didn't belong to Sally."

"Yup. I heard that too."

I picked up my coffee and took a sip. Coming right out with a direct question seemed sort of rude, but I couldn't seem to come up with a way to ease into things. "I guess you'll be getting pretty busy over the holidays now that you're the only bakery in town."

Devita shrugged. "Except for the past few years, I've always been the only bakery on the island."

I nodded. "Yeah. I guess you were."

"Is there a question behind all that stalling?"

I couldn't help but blush. "Not really. It's just that with Sally being your only competitor and all, I just wondered if…"

Devita lifted a brow. "If I killed her to sell a few more cakes?"

I bowed my head. "No, you wouldn't do that. I'm just going to sit down and eat my doughnut. It looks really good."

Devita chuckled but didn't respond.

Well, that was a total failure. I sighed and took a bite of the doughnut. It was really good. I took another bite, then let out an audible sigh. "This is excellent. Are you doing something different with the chocolate?"

"I didn't do anything different, but my partner might have."

"Partner?" I asked.

"I'm getting on in years, so I decided it was time. The best baker I ever met happened to be available, so I jumped at it."

Suddenly, I knew where I'd tasted this specific flavor of chocolate. "Carla."

Devita nodded. "The girl knows her way around a kitchen."

I frowned. "I thought I heard Carla owned part of Sally's shop."

"She did. But she didn't want to run it on her own, so when I offered her a partnership, she took me up on it. Sally's husband is moving back to Seattle and isn't interested in trying to reopen the bakeshop, so Carla worked out the details with his attorney and came into business with me. Seems it worked out well for everyone."

"Except Sally," I pointed out.

"Well, yeah. There is that."

Well, that had turned into an interesting conversation, I thought to myself as I walked back to my car. I wasn't sure if it made Devita more or less a suspect in my mind. This investigation was getting much too complicated for me. I hoped Finn would have something insightful to share when we met that evening.

After I left the bakery, I decided to track down Sue Boatnick. She worked part time for the chamber of commerce as receptionist, so I made a quick right-hand turn and headed in that direction.

"Good afternoon, Sue," I said as I walked through the front door.

"Afternoon, Cait. What brings you out on this windy day?"

"I wanted to ask about the community theater."

Sue smiled. "Are you thinking about helping out with the Christmas play?"

"No. I'll be in Florida for two weeks in December, so that wouldn't work out. I was wondering about a new member of your group. A man named Hugo."

Sue raised a brow. "I'm surprised you're asking about him. He's very good-looking, but didn't I hear you're getting married?"

"I am getting married," I said. "I'm not asking about him because I'm interested in him personally. I'm asking because I heard he might have been seeing Sally before she died."

Sue looked surprised. "Oh, I doubt that. Sally was married and Hugo has a girlfriend."

"Do you know the name of this girlfriend?" I asked.

Sue frowned. "No. It never came up. I just know he lives on San Juan Island. When he decided to join our group, I warned him there would be evenings when rehearsal would run after the ferry stopped running for the day, and he said his girlfriend lived on Madrona Island, so he'd stay with her when he couldn't get home."

"And you never saw him with anyone?"

Sue shook her head. "No. I'm sorry. Is it important?"

"No. Probably not." I turned to leave. "Do you happen to know Hugo's last name?"

"Hugo is his last name. Well, his full name is Antonio Hugoson, but everyone calls him Hugo. If you're really interested in finding out who his girlfriend is, you should ask Summer."

"Summer?" Summer lived down the beach from me but often stayed with Mr. Parsons, along with her husband, Banjo.

"Summer is doing the Christmas play this year. She seems to always know what's going on."

"Okay. Thank you. I'll check with her."

I left the office and headed over to Ship Wreck to see if Summer was in today. Luckily, she was.

"Cait. What are you up to today?"

"I hear you're doing the Christmas play this year."

"I thought it would be fun. I'm going to play the crazy ghost of Christmas present."

Talk about typecasting. "I hear there's a new man in the group. Someone named Hugo."

"Yes. He's going to play Bob Cratchit. He's really very good."

"I've heard as much. I understand he lives on San Juan Island but stays with his girlfriend when he has a late rehearsal."

Summer gave me an odd look. "Yes, that's right. Is there a point to this line of questioning?"

"Do you know who the girlfriend is?"

Summer nodded. "Sure. It's Eve Donner."

Okay, I wasn't expecting that, but I guess it fit. I knew Eve had been on San Juan Island visiting her boyfriend on her days off. She'd also been the one who Sally had supposedly called to cancel the dinner plans she had with the group. Had Eve known her guy was messing around with Sally and confronted her? Had they argued, and had Sally been killed in a fit of rage? Had Eve, who I knew was doing a double shift at the Driftwood on the day the anonymous call came in, tried to set up Miranda to divert attention from herself?

"Thanks, Summer." I hugged her. "I have to go, but you've helped a lot."

Unfortunately, Eve had worked the early shift and had already left for the day by the time I showed up to talk to her. I asked Kimmy about her shift on the

Monday Sally had died and she looked it up for me. Eve had worked the early shift but had taken off a few minutes early. Kimmy remembered Eve saying she had softball practice and then a dinner to get to. I'd have to follow up with her later in the week.

By the time I got home, Cody was at the cabin. From the dark look on his face, I decided talk of the murder investigation could wait until later, when we were all together. Cody had something on his mind, and finding out what was causing his scowl was the most important thing at the moment. It looked like it was going to rain again, so I asked him if he wanted to go with me to take Max out before we went back into town to the grocery store.

"So, is everything ready for the party rental folks to set up tomorrow?" I asked conversationally.

"We're ready. We have the set up tomorrow, the bulk of the cooking on Wednesday, the dinner and the football game on Thursday, and then you and I are going to take a minute to reconnect."

Uh-oh. It sounded like I'd already found the cause of the scowl. "Reconnect?"

Cody blew out a breath that communicated his frustration. "We still haven't set a new wedding date and my mom has been asking about our trip over Christmas. I reminded her that we've been busy with the Thanksgiving feast, but I promise her we'd talk and work things out once it was over."

That sounded fair. "How is she?"

"She seems better. At least she sounds better when I speak to her. She's seen her doctor and had her medications adjusted. She seems calmer. She still doesn't remember everything that happened when she was here, but she said things were beginning to come back to her. She asked me to apologize to you for giving you such a bad time while she was here."

"I appreciate that."

"I'm hoping we can get things back on track and be a family," Cody said. "I'd like our children to grow up spending time with both their grandmothers."

"I want that as well," I said. "Is there something else on your mind?"

"I just can't get past the feeling that my mom really did kill Sally. I don't want to think that, and I'm trying to keep an open mind, but it seems the harder we look for answers, the guiltier she looks."

"I might have picked up another lead. Let's start back and I'll tell you about it."

Chapter 11

It was raining fairly steadily by the time Cody and I made it back into town, but at least the news that I had a strong suspect who wasn't his mother seemed to ease some of the tension from his shoulders. In my mind, Eve had motive to kill Sally and the opportunity to have been the one to make the call to frame Miranda. Now I just needed to prove it.

"I have a list of what we need for the casserole," Cody informed me. "Do we need anything else?"

"Maybe something for dessert."

"How about blackberry pie? I've been craving it ever since I had a piece at the inn when I went to talk to Eric on Friday morning."

"The inn was serving pie?"

"No, but Eric had a pie he'd bought somewhere in town. I was going to…"

"Oh my gosh, if it isn't Cody West!" a loud, high-pitched voice interrupted.

I turned and looked toward the produce aisle.

"Jessica." Cody's startled expression turned into a smile.

I closed my eyes as the girl Cody had dated for most of his junior year in high school captured him in a lip-lock.

"You remember Cait Hart," Cody said after taking a step back.

"Of course. No way I'd forget Danny's little sister."

"I thought you moved to Alabama," Cody said.

"I did. I'm back. Been back since August. I've been meaning to look you up. By the way, how's your mama?"

Cody frowned. "She's good."

Jessica actually looked relieved. "I'm happy to hear that. I was worried after the accident last week."

"Accident?" Cody asked.

Jessica raised a brow. "She didn't tell you?"

"Tell me what?"

"Your mama was standing on the sidewalk out in front of the inn last week when this guy on a bicycle came barreling around the corner and slammed right into her. I was driving by and saw the whole thing. Of course I pulled over and tried to help. The guy on the bike had a huge gash on his arm that was bleeding like crazy. By the time I parked and made my way over to them, the blood from his cut was all over the front of your mama's clothes. I nearly died when I thought the blood was hers. I helped her sit up and realized the blood was his. Talk about relieved. She didn't look hurt, so I helped her to her feet. She insisted she was fine, but she seemed dazed and confused. I asked her if I should call you, or maybe take her to the emergency room, but she said no, that she'd just had the wind knocked out of her. She told me she was staying at the inn and would just go inside and lay down. I felt so bad. So did the guy on the bike. He offered to pay for her dry cleaning because her pretty pink sweater was all but ruined, but she said it was old and she'd just put it in the washer."

"When exactly was this?" I asked.

Jessica glanced at me. She put a finger to her chin. "I was on my way home from the dentist, so it must have been Monday of last week."

"And what time would you say it was?" I inquired.

"I guess around three forty or three forty-five. My appointment was over at three thirty and I was driving home, so it would have been around then. Why?"

"We're trying to put together a timeline for my mother of Monday," Cody said. "She had a mix-up with her medication and wasn't feeling well for much of the day."

Jessica put her hand to her chest. "The poor thing. I knew something was off. She didn't even recognize me at first, and we were so close back when I lived here and we were dating. I guess I should have followed up on my hunch and called you after all."

"I understand why you might not have if Mom asked you not to," Cody said. "And it all worked out in the end. It does explain where she got the blood on her clothing. As it turned out, she didn't remember when I asked her about it."

"Oh, the poor dear." Jessica grabbed Cody by the hand. "That must have been so frightening for her. Is she still in town?"

"No. She's gone home."

"I'm sorry I missed the chance to catch up with her. By the way, I hear congratulations are in order."

She looked at me. "I always thought there was a spark between the two of you. Even back then. I'm happy you finally found each other."

"Thank you," I said. I felt like I should say more, but I wasn't sure what. The woman was nice enough, and she seemed genuinely happy that Cody and I were getting married, but I couldn't help but be a bit jealous when I considered how long they'd dated.

Cody chatted with Jessica a while longer and then we continued with our shopping. I was relieved that the blood on his mother's clothes had been explained, and it did seem that if Jessica saw her at three forty-five and Sally had a customer at three fifty-five, it proved Mrs. West hadn't been the one to kill her.

******

"That casserole was delicious," Siobhan said after the sleuthing gang had finished the dinner Cody and I had prepared.

"It was mostly Cody's doing, but it did turn out well," I answered.

"I bet the cheese sauce you poured over the top would be delicious over vegetables," Siobhan said. "Maybe broccoli or cauliflower."

"It would be worth trying," I agreed. "Speaking of veggies, has anyone spoken to Francine today? I meant to stop by to see if she needed anything, but then I got busy."

"I spoke to her," Tara said. "Everything is on track. She's very organized. If things go according to plan, there should be very little cooking to be done on Thursday."

"I agree," Siobhan said. "Francine even told me she was planning to watch the Macy's Thanksgiving Day Parade with Mr. Parsons, Banjo, and Summer. She figured it would be a good idea to relax in the morning because the afternoon would be hectic."

"Are you both planning to play in the football game?" I asked. "Cody and I are."

"Yes, we are," Siobhan said. "I think Michael and Maggie are keeping score. Mom is coming as a spectator and will keep an eye on Connor."

"I'm going to be there, but I'm not planning to play," Tara said. "Unless they just need a body. Danny said it was going to be close in terms of having a full team. I can't throw or catch, but I can stand around to fill out the team."

"I'm playing," Cassie volunteered. "I'm looking forward to making mincemeat out of the gang from Shots."

"Speaking of mincemeat," Cody said, "Mr. Parsons requested a mincemeat pie. Francine said she'd make sure she made a couple just for him."

"It really is sweet the way she looks out for him," Siobhan said. "The way you both do."

"Mr. Parsons is a very special man. It's my privilege to be part of his life."

Once the dishes were done, we gathered around the whiteboard. Now that Cody's mom was definitely cleared, I wondered if I even wanted to continue. It was a question I'd been asking myself a lot with this particular case. For some reason, it was really wearing on me.

"Okay, who can we clear?" Siobhan began.

"Eli Alderman," Finn said. "I spoke to Sheriff Fowler today. He was able to verify Eli's whereabouts during the death window and he definitely isn't our guy."

"So that leaves Nick Enderling, Devita Colter, and the person who made the purchase at the bakery at three fifty-five," Siobhan said.

"We can eliminate Nick Enderling as well," Finn said. "I guess I haven't mentioned that his presence in Virginia has been verified. He couldn't have killed Sally."

"And then there were two," Tara said.

"We don't really think Devita Colter killed Sally, do we?" Siobhan asked.

"She did have motive," I pointed out. "I don't think she did it. Although…"

"Although?" Cassie asked.

"She was kind of odd when I spoke to her."

"Odd how?" Cassie pushed.

"I'm not sure. Just satisfied, I'd say, with the way things worked out. I guess in a way she should be. Her only competition is gone and she has a new partner with mad baking skills and youthful energy. But still, it didn't seem quite right to be as happy as she was, given Sally's dead. I don't necessarily think she did it, but I'd leave her on the list."

Siobhan took a step back from the board. "Okay, so we have Devita Colter and the person who bought the cookies at three fifty-five. There has to be a way to figure out who that person was. Someone must have seen someone going in or out of the bakery."

I looked at Finn. "Maybe you should speak to Miranda again."

"Miranda?"

"It occurred to me to ask her if she had any idea why she was set up. Why not one of the other suspects? Why Miranda?"

"That's a good question, and one I've asked myself," Finn said. "When I last spoke to Miranda, she didn't seem to know why anyone would want to frame her. She insisted she didn't have any enemies and was certain she must have been selected by the killer to take the fall due to nothing more than proximity. But when I was speaking to her, I sensed something more. Something she wasn't saying. I couldn't get it out of her, but maybe you can."

"I'll talk to her tomorrow," I said. "You'd think if someone had tried to frame her and she suspected who it was, she'd want to have that person arrested."

"Perhaps," Finn said. "Or maybe the person who framed her knows something that would get her into trouble. Not necessarily for Sally's death, but for something else. It's hard to say, but I won't be surprised if we find she's involved in some way."

"It would be a real twist if the killer knew they were a suspect so they sloppily framed themselves, knowing the evidence would show they were framed, which would seem to eliminate them as a suspect, even though they were guilty," I said.

Finn frowned. "Yes, that would be a twist."

Cassie laughed. "Your mind works in mysterious ways."

I shrugged and picked up Cosmo. "Okay, kitty. I came up with a funny twist to this mystery, but I think it's time for you to come up with the killer."

"Meow."

"I seriously need to learn to speak cat," I said.

"Oh, I think you do pretty well most of the time," Tara countered.

I cuddled the cat to my chest and gave his neck a rub. It really had taken a lot of the pressure off now that we knew Cody's mom was absolutely, positively off the hook. "By the way," I said to Finn, "what was Sheriff Fowler's reaction when you told him about our conversation with Jessica?"

"He was reserved. Of course, he has to speak to her himself. Unless Sally was killed a lot earlier than we thought, and the purchase at three fifty-five was bogus, there's very little chance Mrs. West could be guilty."

I suspected the others, like me, were ready to move on from this murder case. I decided to introduce a lighter subject while I worked through the thought that was nagging at the back of my mind. "When I told Danny this afternoon that Cody and I had run into Jessica, he told me a funny story about a Thanksgiving prank when Cody, Danny, and Jessica were in the eleventh grade."

Cody groaned. "We don't need to go there. Talk about embarrassing."

"I remember that." Siobhan laughed.

I sat back and smiled. My distraction seemed to have worked. Siobhan, of course, was ignoring Cody's pleas not to go on, and we were all laughing at the stupid things teens sometimes do in the face of a dare. It did my heart good to see everyone relaxed, though when I finally figured out what it was that had been nagging at me, my smile was replaced with a frown.

Chapter 12

Tuesday, November 20

I wasn't sure how well my attempt to maintain a neutral expression was coming off. From the meaningful glances Cody was sending my way, I'd have to say not all that well. He asked several times if something was wrong, and I replied that I was just going over the plans for the Thanksgiving dinner in my mind to ensure we didn't forget anything and weren't left scrambling at the last minute. I had a sick feeling I had figured out who had framed Miranda Wells, but I wanted to check it out before I said anything to him.

Cody left to see to the delivery of the rented tables and chairs and I headed into town. When I arrived at the Driftwood Café, I was happy to see Alice was once again manning the desk.

"Morning, Cait. Are you here for breakfast?"

"Actually, I just had one more question for you. We spoke about the customers who were here last

Thursday and you gave me a list of everyone who was dining at around three o'clock. Was there anyone here to pick up takeout?"

Alice paused. "There was one man. I didn't recognize him. I don't think he was local."

"What did he buy?"

"A blackberry pie. It was our special that day."

I felt my heart melt into my stomach. "Did you at any point leave the reception desk while he was waiting?"

Alice nodded. "Sure. I went to the kitchen to box up the pie. I was gone for maybe three minutes. Is there a problem?"

I shook my head. "No. No problem. Do you remember when the man came in?"

"Not specifically. Maybe thirty minutes into my shift."

I glanced at the telephone sitting on the desk. I had a feeling I knew who had framed Miranda. Now I just needed to tell my fiancé that while his mother was innocent, he had a relative who might not be. The only detail that cast any doubt on my theory was that Eric wasn't a woman.

******

"So, did you talk to your cousin?" I asked Cody that afternoon, after I'd explained my theory to him, completely demolishing his recently acquired good mood.

Cody ran a hand through his hair. "Yeah." He let out a breath. "I spoke to him."

"And?"

"And he admitted to making the call and planting the rolling pin in Miranda's shop."

I put a hand to my chest. "Why would he do that?"

"Eric believed at that point that my mom was guilty. She'd been acting oddly, and he found her clothes with blood on them. When I came by the inn and confronted her about the medications she was taking, Eric realized her behavior might have been his fault because he was the one who'd given her the pills. He knew he needed to get them both off the island, but Mom had been ordered to stay put by the sheriff. He figured if he had someone else to focus his investigation on, he'd be diverted from looking too closely at Mom."

"I guess that makes sense, but why Miranda, and why use the phone at the Driftwood?"

Cody looked so tired. I felt so bad for him. "Eric had overheard people at the inn talking about Miranda, and that she was a strong suspect in the case. He figured she'd be believable as the killer, so he planted the rolling pin in her storage room. He hadn't planned to make the call from the Driftwood, but he didn't want to use a phone that could be traced back to him. When he stopped by to get the pie, and saw the place was all but deserted, he decided to jump on the opportunity when he was left alone with the phone. He disguised his voice and called in the anonymous tip."

I sat down next to Cody. "So what do we do? Do we tell Finn?"

Cody rested his elbows on his knees and put his head in his hands. "I don't know. I suppose we should, but I'm hesitant. Eric has always been a jerk, but he did it to help my mother. He really thought she was guilty. Heck, so did I. The idea of sneaking her off the island entered my mind more than once, so I understand why Eric did it. Of course, I'd never try to pin the murder on someone else."

I wasn't sure what to say. If we told Finn what Eric had done, he might be arrested for tampering with an investigation. And maybe he should be. On the other hand, it had been proven that the rolling pin wasn't the murder weapon, so Miranda was off the hook. Finn needed to know, but I decided to let Cody come around to that conclusion on his own.

Cody needed to get back to Mr. Parsons's to meet the delivery people. I decided to give him some space to work through things in his mind, so I went into town to try to figure out the rest of this mystery. We knew who'd framed Miranda; now we just needed to find out who'd killed Sally.

******

After two hours of walking up and down the street where Sally's bakery was located, talking to folks who'd claimed not to have noticed anything unusual the day Sally died, I was getting pretty frustrated. And then I happened to run into one of the pressers who worked for Oliver Patton in the alley behind the cleaners, and things began to slide into place.

"Yikes. I can see I'm busted." Laura Riverton slipped the cigarette in her hand behind her back. "You won't tell, will you? Oliver has a strict policy about not smoking while on shift, but there's no way I can make it eight hours without a fix. I slip out here a couple of times a day when no one's looking."

"Your secret is safe with me," I assured her. It was freezing and damp today, so if she was willing to brave the elements for a smoke, she must really need it.

"Thanks." Laura looked at the object between her fingers. "Nasty habit, but a heck of a hard one to break."

"So I've heard." I looked up and down the alley. There was a single back door, but it didn't appear to line up directly with the dry cleaners. "Does that back door lead to the cleaners?" I asked.

"It leads to the hallway shared by the four businesses in the building. The alley access is supposed to be used for deliveries, but I'm not the only person who uses it for a quick nicotine fix."

I glanced at the door again. "So you can get to any of the four businesses through that door?"

"Sure. That's what I just said."

"And are the doors leading from the hallway into each of the businesses kept locked?"

"Not during business hours. I think the hallway is supposed to provide an emergency exit as well."

"So as an employee of the dry cleaners, you have backdoor access to the bakery or trinket shop?"

Laura frowned. "Sure, I guess. Why are you asking all these questions?"

I blushed. "Sorry. I just had a thought I wanted to confirm. Listen, I have to go. Enjoy your smoke."

Making a quick decision, I went directly to Finn's office. Yes, there was a part of me who wanted to confront Miranda directly to test out my theory, but I had enough on my plate this week without foolishly putting myself in danger. When I arrived at the storefront next to the newspaper where Finn kept his office, I found him alone.

"I have to say, you look like a woman with a mission if ever there was one." Finn chuckled. "I take it you have news."

"I do have news." I looked toward the hallway that led to the private office. "Are you alone? Can we talk in confidence?"

"I'm alone. What's up?"

"I think I know who killed Sally."

Finn motioned for me to take a seat across the desk from him. "Okay. Who killed Sally?"

"Miranda Wells."

"Miranda Wells has been cleared," Finn reminded me.

"Not necessarily. Remember my crazy theory about Miranda being guilty but wanting to divert attention from her actions on the day of the murder and so framing herself with evidence she knew would be proven false, thereby making it appear as if she wasn't guilty at all?"

"You think Miranda framed herself?" Finn asked.

"No. She didn't frame herself. Someone else framed her, but what if the actions of the person who framed her led to the same thing? What if Miranda really did kill Sally? She definitely had motive, means, and opportunity. She was a serious suspect until she was arrested based on false evidence. Then, suddenly, she was off the hook simply because the evidence used to arrest her turned out to be fake."

Finn frowned. "Okay, I'm following. But why are you so set on Miranda as the killer? Do you have proof?"

"No, I don't have proof. But I do have a theory."

"I'm listening."

"I was canvassing the area near the bakeshop today when I ran into one of the pressers who works for Oliver Patton. She was in the alley, having a smoke. As we chatted, I noticed for the first time that there's a back door leading from the building out into the alley. The door is used for deliveries and services for all four businesses in the building. I realized that gave Miranda access to the bakery without her having to go out onto the sidewalk in the front of the building."

Finn looked a bit confused but still open to what I was saying. "Okay. Keep going."

"Several people saw Mrs. West yelling at Sally. We still don't know exactly when she left, but we do know she was in an accident in front of the inn at around three forty-five, so she probably would have had to leave the bakery by three thirty at the very latest to get there. I'm guessing earlier, around three fifteen or three twenty. I know two witnesses claimed to have seen Mrs. West yelling at Sally at three thirty, but they admitted they weren't sure of the exact time, and it does seem as if Sally wouldn't have put up with being yelled at for a full thirty minutes, so three fifteen to three thirty seems to make a better estimate."

"Okay. Where are you going with this?"

"Hang on. I got sidetracked, I guess, but I'm almost there. Based on the charge entered into the register at three fifty-five, we've been placing the time of death at four o'clock."

"Yes, that's what we're using as time of death."

"Which give Miranda an alibi, because she had customers from around four o'clock to four thirty.

But what if the time of death is off? What if Mrs. West left at or before three thirty and Miranda snuck over via the shared hallway and confronted her about her plot to take over her lease right after that? What if that's when the confrontation became violent and Sally ended up on the receiving end of a rolling pin to the head? What if Miranda knew she would be a suspect and would need an alibi, so she rang up the fake sale at three fifty-five and returned to her shop by four o'clock? She has receipts to show she rang up sales of her own between four and four thirty. And she might have. Or those sales might be fake too."

"That's a good theory, but how do we prove it?" Finn asked. "When we searched her place after the anonymous tip, we didn't find anything other than the planted rolling pin, which means if she is guilty, she was smart enough to get rid of any real evidence."

"Yeah," I admitted. "Finding proof might be a problem." I smiled at Finn. "But it's your job to prove these things, and I have a dinner to get ready for, so I'll leave you to it."

"Cait…" Finn said as I got up to leave.

"Yes?"

"You now seem certain Miranda didn't plant the fake evidence even though it was your crazy theory that she might have in the first place. Why are you so certain?"

"Because I know who did it."

"Who?"

"Give me until the end of the day and I'll fill you in. I have someone I need to talk to first."

I returned to the cabin as soon as I left Finn's office. Cody still wasn't there, so I went to the main house to check in with Siobhan and Maggie. The wonderful smell of pumpkin alerted me to the fact that they were baking pies before I entered.

"It smells amazing in here." I poured a cup of coffee and sat down at the kitchen table.

"We decided to do pies today and the turkey and sides tomorrow," Siobhan said.

"It seems like everything is right on track," I commented after taking a sip of hot brew.

"I think we're in good shape. Francine is really on top of things," Maggie said. "We may end up with enough food to feed several small armies, but I suppose we can send everyone home with leftover bags."

"How did the sleuthing go?" Siobhan asked.

I filled her in on my theory of Miranda as the killer, and that I'd told everything to Finn and left it in his capable hands. "Now all I need to do is get my wedding back on track and I'll be able to relax and enjoy the holidays."

"Have you heard anything about when the church is supposed to reopen?" Siobhan asked as she slid a pie into the oven.

"Not until mid-December. That's when Cody and I are leaving for Florida, and we really wanted to be married before we went. I guess we'll need to look for a new venue."

"Is Cody's mom planning to come back?" Siobhan asked.

"No. We've talked about it, and given the circumstances, we're going to get married without her. She mentioned doing a reception of some sort for her family and friends when we get to Florida."

"What about having it here?" Siobhan suggested.

"I doubt everyone will fit."

"So don't invite everyone. Do something really intimate. Only invite the people you and Cody absolutely need to have at your wedding to be happy," Siobhan said. "I'm not saying who you *should* invite, or who Mom wanted to invite, just the people you and Cody absolutely need."

"Well, you and Finn, of course, and Maggie and Michael, Mom and Gabe, Cassie, Danny, and Aiden, and Aiden will want to bring Alanna." I paused and caught my breath. "And of course Tara and Mr. Parsons. I'd like to invite Francine, as well as Banjo and Summer. Oh, and Willow and Alex." I paused again. "And Marley."

"Is there anyone else you simply must have?"

"I'll need to check with Cody, but no, I guess that's it if we're talking family and close friends only."

Siobhan used her fingers to come up with a number. "Counting you and Cody, that's twenty," Siobhan pointed out. "We've had twenty to dinner before."

"Oh, and Sister Mary," I added, referring to Tara's biological mother.

"Okay, twenty-one."

I paused to let the idea sink in. I really did want to get this whole wedding thing behind me, and a small ceremony seemed preferable to going to city hall, which I'd started to seriously consider. I smiled. "I'll need to run this past Cody, but I like it. When, though?"

"How about tomorrow?" Siobhan suggested. "You're scheduled to go back to work on Friday, which is the first day of your busiest season. Why not be married before you return?"

"Cody and I have the marriage license, but we'll need to find someone to officiate. Father Bartholomew wouldn't do it here in the house."

"What about Michael?" Maggie suggested.

"Michael can still do weddings?"

"He's no longer a priest, so he can't perform traditional Catholic weddings, but he's still licensed by the State of Washington."

That sounded perfect, and I said so, then texted Cody to let him know we needed to talk right away. He met me at the house immediately. By the time we'd talked things through, we'd come up with a final list of twenty-five guests. Cody seemed almost relieved with the decision to get married here at the house tomorrow evening and then have a dinner together in place of a reception. Michael confirmed that he was delighted to perform the ceremony, and Maggie and Siobhan promised to take care of everything else, so I called Tara and then went back into town to get my hair trimmed and my nails manicured.

Chapter 13

Wednesday, November 21

"You look beautiful," Siobhan said as I stood in front of the mirror and considered my image. I peered at the dress Maggie had so lovingly made for me, through eyes made up by Siobhan to look natural yet defined. I held the bouquet Cassie had made from flowers she'd handpicked for the occasion. Around my neck was the sapphire necklace Tara had given me for my something blue. I wore the garter my mother had worn when she married my father for the something borrowed, and the dress Maggie had made featured small pearls that had originally been sewn onto the dress worn by my grandmother for the something old.

I smiled in response because I knew if I opened my mouth the tears I was holding back would spill down my face despite my best intentions. I couldn't believe the wedding I'd spent a year avoiding was finally here. Everything had been such a huge mess, and on the surface, it seemed as if Cody and I had both made compromises. But now I knew in my heart this small wedding with those closest to us would be absolutely perfect.

"Once the music starts, we're going to walk down the stairs to where the guys are waiting in the living room," Siobhan explained. "Cassie will go first and stand next to Aiden, I'll go next and stand next to Finn, and Tara will come down just before you and stand next to Danny. Once Tara's in place, the music will change and you'll come down the stairs slowly so we can get photos. Mr. Parsons is going to meet you at the bottom of the stairs and walk you the rest of the way down the aisle. He'll kiss your cheek, then hand you over to Cody. Any questions?"

I shook my head.

"Are you okay?" Tara asked.

I took a deep breath. "I'm fine. I'm just trying not to cry. I'd hate to mess up the makeup Siobhan spent hours getting just right."

Siobhan hugged me. "Cry if you need to. I used professional-grade cosmetics. If you're trapped outdoors in a hurricane, you can be assured your mascara won't run."

I couldn't help but laugh as I wiped away a single tear that streamed down my face but, as promised, didn't cause the makeup to run.

"Mom wanted a minute alone with you," Siobhan said. "I can hear her in the hall. We'll be waiting for you at the top of the stairs."

I nodded again. Siobhan, Cassie, and Tara walked out as my mother came in. She put her hand to her mouth as tears streamed down her face.

"You look so beautiful."

I choked back more tears. "Thank you. I can't believe this moment is finally here."

Mom faced me and took my hands in hers. "That's the way life works most of the time. We spend much of the time we have on this earth planning for the big events. Births, weddings, anniversaries, trips. Then, in the blink of an eye, they're over." Mom ran a finger down my cheek. "I remember my own wedding. How scared I was and yet how happy. As I looked into the future, I believed the world was mine. And it was. For a while. Your dad and I had a wonderful life. We bore five beautiful children. He would be so proud of you, as am I."

"I miss him," I said as another tear escaped down my cheek.

"I know. I do too. I'm sorry he isn't here to share this with you." Mom touched her hand to her chest. "But I know he's with you in spirit."

I leaned forward and hugged my mom. She hugged me back and then took a step back.

"Today is a day for happy tears, not sad ones. I have something for you." Mom handed me a box.

I opened it and gasped. Inside were gorgeous diamond earrings. "They're beautiful."

"I wore these on my wedding day. There was a matching necklace, which I gave to Siobhan when she married, and a bracelet, which I'll give to Cassie when her time comes. They were my mother's."

I hugged Mom again. "Thank you so much."

Mom kissed my cheek. "I'm going to go downstairs. Gabe is waiting for me. I'll see you in a bit."

My heart was pounding as I slipped the earrings onto my lobes. I'd have to be careful not to lose them—they were clip-ons, not studs—but the fact that I had a piece of my mother and my grandmother that I could someday hand down to my own daughter meant the world to me. I could hear the sound of music as Tara slipped her head in around the door.

"Are you ready?"

I nodded. "More than ready."

Although I hadn't been able to get married in the church, as I'd always dreamed, the ceremony was perfect. Mr. Parsons looked so handsome in his suit, and the smile in his eyes confirmed that I'd been right to ask him to be part of this special day. Tara, Siobhan, and Cassie cried throughout the entire ceremony, but somehow I was able to get through it without shedding any more tears.

After the vows were exchanged, Cody and I took a minute to ourselves in one of the upstairs guest rooms before heading down to the dinner Siobhan and Tara had spent half the day preparing.

"We did it." I smiled as I gazed into Cody's eyes.

He smiled back at me. "We did. You look amazing."

I looped my arms around his neck. He leaned forward and kissed me.

"Somewhere in my heart, I always knew I was going to marry you," Cody whispered against my lips.

I pulled back just a bit and raised a brow. "*Always*? I seem to remember quite the parade of girls between the day we first met and now."

Cody shrugged. "You were too young. I was too young. My mind told me to wait, but my heart knew." Cody ran a finger down my cheek. "I've always loved you and I always will. I can't wait to make a life with you."

The tears I'd been holding back were released all at once. "And I can't wait to make a life with you. I think, Cody West, we're going to be amazing."

Chapter 14

Thursday, November 22

When I'd suggested the football game between O'Malley's and Shots be held at ten o'clock in the morning, I hadn't been aware that the night before would be my wedding night. To say that my tank was running on half empty was an understatement, but Cody and I had promised to be there, so we'd rolled ourselves out of bed, taken long showers, and downed a couple of pots of coffee.

"Your face is crooked." Cassie laughed.

"Crooked?" I asked.

"You still have the fake eyelash Siobhan glued on for the wedding on your right eye, but the one on your left eye is gone."

I groaned. "Terrific. I tried to take them off this morning when I showered, but they were glued on tight, so I left them on to keep from ripping my real eyelashes out. I guess the one on the left must have loosened enough to give way at some point." I looked around for my older sister. "I wonder if Siobhan has anything in her purse that will remove the lashes that refused to wash away."

"I'm betting she does. She's over near the parking lot, talking to Maggie and Michael. I'll go ask her for you."

I smiled at my younger sister. "Thanks. That would be great."

I looked toward the field, where Cody was chatting with Aiden, Danny, and Finn. I imagined they were coming up with a plan of attack. Initially, I'd been enthusiastic about the game, but the pounding headache I couldn't quite get rid of had me wishing I'd called in sick and stayed in bed.

I waved at Danny, who gestured me over.

"You look like hell," he said with a grin.

"Bite me."

"I'd say we put Cait on tackle because she seems to have the disposition to go with the role, but this is flag football. Can you handle blocking?"

I nodded. "I can handle any job you give me."

Cody took me by the shoulders and turned me so that we were facing each other. "What happened to your eye?"

I put my hand to my face. "Nothing. It's fine." I glanced at Cassie and Siobhan, who were coming in my direction. "Just give me a couple of minutes and I'll be good to go."

I could hear Danny and Aiden chuckling while Cody looked confused. I had a feeling this was going to be one of those days when I found myself wishing I only had sisters. Brothers could be a real pain in the butt.

******

"Great game and great catch, which has earned you a very highly sought-after victory cookie," said Libby Baldwin, Danny and Aiden's twenty-one-year-old cocktail waitress who'd recently found out she was pregnant and so was forced to watch from the sidelines.

"Thank you." I accepted a familiar-looking turkey-shaped cookie from Libby. "Is Devita making these cookies now that Carla's working for her?"

"No, I bought them from Sally before she died. At the time I purchased them, I had no idea they'd be the last turkey-shaped cookies Sally would make. When I found out she'd been killed shortly after I left the bakery, I decided to freeze them and bring them to the Thanksgiving game as rewards for a job well done. It's my way of participating. Of course, I only have a dozen cookies and I ate three before I had the idea to save them, so I'm only giving cookies to those who made a significant contribution, and your catch made the cut."

I frowned as I stared at the cookie. "You bought these cookies on the Monday Sally was murdered?"

Libby's smile faded, and suddenly she looked uncertain. "Yes. Was it insensitive of me to bring them here? Did I mess up? I wasn't trying to appear callous, I just thought the turkey cookie rewards would be cute."

"What time did you buy the cookies?"

Libby took a step back. "Is something wrong? Should I put the rest of the cookies in my car?"

I took a breath and let it out. "No. I'm sorry. Your idea was lovely. I've been trying to firm up a timeline for what happened between three and four o'clock on Monday, November 12, and I've been missing the part relating to a purchase made at three fifty-five."

Libby hesitated and then answered. "I guess that's about when I was there."

"And Sally helped you?"

Libby nodded. "She said I was going to be the last sale of the day because she had a dinner to get to and needed to lock up."

"And were you the only one in the bakery when you made your purchase?"

"Actually, I heard Sally talking to a man when I first walked in. They were in the kitchen, so I couldn't see who it was, but he had a deep voice and an accent."

"Did you hear what they were talking about?"

"No. Sally came out to the front after I walked in. No one else came in while I was there, but a woman walked in through the back door just as I was leaving."

"What woman? Do you know her name?"

"I don't know her name, but she works at the Driftwood Café. I've seen her in there a bunch of times."

"Eve? Is her name Eve?"

Libby frowned. "I think it might be."

I hugged Libby. "Thanks. You've been very helpful." I looked around. "Have you seen Finn?"

"He was heading to the parking lot."

I took off at a jog in that direction. Finn was just getting into his car when I arrived.

"Wait," I said.

"What is it? I need to go. The subpoena to search Miranda Wells's home again has just come through.

It wasn't easy to get because we'd already searched the place."

"It wasn't Miranda. At least, I don't think it was. I think it was Eve Donner."

"Eve? Why do you think Eve killed Sally?"

"Because Libby Baldwin just told me that she was the person to who bought cookies at three fifty-five on the day Sally died, and as she was leaving, Eve was walking in. I also heard Sally may have been sleeping with Eve's boyfriend. And to top it off, Connie Salisman told me that Eve told her group, who were meeting for dinner that night, that Sally called her to cancel, but Sally told Libby she needed to close up in a hurry because she had a dinner to get to."

Finn frowned. "Are you sure about all this? Two days ago you were sure it was Miranda who killed Sally."

"I'm sure."

"We're going to need proof."

I nodded. "I have a plan. Give me a minute to let Cody know I'm going with you on an errand and I'll fill you in."

******

"This has to be one of your crazier ideas," Finn said twenty minutes later as he drove toward Eve's house. I just hoped she was home and not spending the holiday on San Juan Island with her cheating boyfriend.

"It's not a crazy idea. It's a very good one. We know Eve will most likely not speak to you or allow you to search her car or her house, and we'll never get a warrant on Thanksgiving, but there's no reason for her not to talk to me."

"I'm not sure about you going inside alone."

I took out my phone. "I told you, I won't be alone. I'm going to call you before I go in. You're going to answer so we make sure we have a connection. Then I'm going to accidentally forget to hang up before sticking the phone in my pocket. We might not be able to get a warrant for a search or a wiretap, but no one can fault you for giving your sister-in-law a ride to a friend's and then waiting out front for her to talk to that friend. And a phone line accidentally left open isn't at all like wearing a wire. We're good. If Eve goes all Rambo on me and I need saving, you can rush in on your white horse."

Finn groaned. "Cody is going to kill me if I get his new wife killed the day after the wedding."

"You won't have to worry about Cody. Siobhan will kill you first. If I get into trouble, just don't be late with the rescue."

Finn, who was driving his civilian car and not his cruiser, pulled up just down the street from Eve's house. I could see he wasn't happy about any of this, but he knew me well enough to realize I wasn't going to let this go.

"What's your plan exactly?" Finn asked. "Are you just going to go inside and ask Eve if she killed Sally?"

I shrugged. "I don't know. Maybe. We suspected Sally had been hit over the head with a rolling pin, but Kimmy told me that Eve was on her way to softball practice after she got off work that day, so I'm thinking Eve killed her with a bat. I'm hoping it will be sitting in plain sight for me to find."

"Unlikely."

I bit my lip. "Yeah. I guess it *is* unlikely. I guess I'll just wing it."

I called Finn's phone and established a connection, then slipped my phone into the pocket of my sweatshirt. I opened the car door and slipped out. "Wish me luck."

As I walked down the sidewalk to the path leading up to the house, I found myself wishing I had more of a plan than I did, but it seemed plans hadn't been working out anyway lately, so what the heck.

I knocked on the door and waited.

"Cait? What are you doing here?" Eve's roommate, Rena, asked.

"I came to see Eve. Is she here?"

"No. She's on San Juan Island with Hugo. She won't be home until Sunday."

"Drat. She borrowed my iPad the other day and I wanted to get it back. I don't suppose she left her softball bag here?"

"It's in her car. But her car is here. Hugo picked her up."

"Do you have a key? My recipe for stuffing is on that iPad, and maybe you've heard, I'm throwing a huge dinner later today. I really need that recipe."

Rena turned and looked behind her. "She usually leaves her keys in the bowl near the back door. Let me check."

I followed Rena into the house and down the hallway. Sure enough, there was a set of keys in the bowl. Rena picked them up, looking momentarily uncertain.

"Do you think you can check her car for her bag? It would help me out a bunch."

Rena shrugged. "Yeah. Okay. There's nothing worse than trying to make a meal without your recipes." She headed out the back door to the car. "I heard you invited a bunch of people without families to this event. I think that's really nice."

"It started as a Christmas Eve celebration for our friend Mr. Parsons, but it's really taken off."

Rena looked in through the window. The back seat was empty, so she popped the trunk. Laying across the bottom of the trunk was a black bag. Rena unzipped it and pulled it open. She frowned.

"What is it?" I asked.

Rena held up a bat. "Eve's bat. It looks like it has blood on it."

Chapter 15

"What a great turnout," Francine said as the two of us stood watching the almost hundred guests who had ended up attending our feast chow down.

"It is a great turnout. More than we were expecting, and we're still going to have too much food."

"I bought a bunch of takeout containers. Anyone who wants to can make up a meal to take with them once everyone has had their fill."

I smiled. "You're a really good hostess."

Francine shrugged. "I enjoy entertaining. Not that I do much anymore, but this has been fun. I spoke to Mr. Parsons, and I think we're going to go ahead and throw a smaller event at Christmas."

"Oh, that's a great idea. I'm sorry I'm going to miss it."

"We'll miss you and Cody as well. But maybe next year." Francine glanced at the buffet table. "It looks like I need to set out more gravy."

After she walked away, Finn walked over to me. "Is everything buttoned up?" I asked.

He nodded. "The sheriff picked Eve up and has her in custody, and he sent one of his deputies over to pick up the softball bag and bat, which he shuffled off to the crime lab. He didn't even ask very many questions about how my sister-in-law just happened to be looking inside Eve's bag even though Eve wasn't on the island."

I smiled. "See? I told you it would all work out."

"I spoke to Cody about Eric."

I looked down. "And?"

"And he'll need to answer for his role in attempting to frame Miranda. I've shared what I know with the sheriff and he's going to have the police in Florida near where Eric lives talk to him. He won't do any serious time. He might even get off with a slap on the wrist and probation. It's out of my hands now."

"I'm glad Cody told you himself. I would have if he hadn't, but I suspected he'd do the right thing once he had a chance to think things through." I glanced at my new husband, who was chatting with Mr. Parsons and a few others. "At least he seems happy today."

"I think he is happy. Turning Eric in couldn't have been easy, and I'm sure his mother is furious. When I spoke to Cody earlier, he said the trip to Florida was in question now because his mother isn't speaking to him anymore. She's basically disowned him."

"That's so unfair," I said.

"I agree. Cody did the right thing. It was Eric who made the wrong move. I'm not sure how much of this Cody plans to tell you. At least today. But I wanted you to know. I think he's a bit fragile right now. It might be up to you to cheer him up."

I smiled. "I think I can handle that."

Finn winked at me. "I know you can." He looked around the room. "Have you seen my lovely wife?"

"Last I saw, she was in the kitchen."

Finn left, and I made the rounds, stopping to speak briefly to everyone. When I arrived at Chappy's table, I saw he had a plate full of yams and a cat in his lap. "I see you met Cosmo."

"He came over to say hi. Seems he likes yams almost as much as I do."

The cat did look content.

"Is this cat one of your strays?" Chappy asked.

I paused before I answered. I supposed at this point he was. We'd solved the case and his job was done. He'd shuffled the clues in my direction, even though I'd only understood them in hindsight. Even the fact that he'd been sitting in front of the Driftwood Café had been a clue that had blown right over my head. "He isn't exactly a stray, but he's looking for a good home. Are you interested?" Usually, the magical cats found homes with children or people in emotional or physical need. Chappy was getting on in years, and he did live alone. I imagined he was as much in need of a faithful companion as anyone.

"I guess I might be. If he's agreeable, of course."

I looked at the cat. "How about it, Cosmo? Are you interested in rooming with Chappy?"

"Meow." The cat began to purr so loudly, everyone nearby looked in his direction.

I looked at Chappy. "It looks like you just found yourself a roommate. I'll send food and supplies home with you. Don't forget them."

Chappy grinned. "I won't forget. I think Cosmo and I will have a good life together."

I smiled back. I was sure they would at that. It did my heart good when things worked out. I glanced at all the people I loved. Mom had Gabe now, and Maggie had Michael. Aiden had Alanna, and Siobhan had Finn and Connor. I had Cody, and in a strange, platonic way, Mr. Parsons had Francine, and of course Alex had Willow and Barry. Cassie was still single, but she was barely out of high school. And Tara? I'd been hoping and praying she would find her one and only, but when I saw her sitting next to Danny with a huge grin on her face, I had to admit my smile turned to a frown. Would those two ever be done with each other?

Up Next from Kathi Daley Books

Preview:

Maybe it *had* been insanity that caused me to sell my condo, pack my belongings, and buy a huge old house I had never even seen. Maybe it *had* been my unwillingness to face the grief I *would* not deal with and *could* not escape, that caused me to move to a town I knew nothing about and had never even visited. Or maybe, just maybe, when I'd seen the ad for the rundown old house perched on a bluff overlooking the sea, I hadn't been running at all. Maybe, I tried desperately to convince myself, I'd simply seen the opportunity to do something fun. Creative. Different.

No, I admitted as I gingerly placed a foot on the first of three rotted steps leading to the decayed front porch. It hadn't been insanity, an unwillingness to deal, or a longing for fun that caused me to give up my life in California to move to a tiny town in coastal Maine where no one knew who I was or what I had been through. What it had been, I decided, was preservation.

I sighed in relief when I made it to the front door without falling through the rotted wood. I took out the brand-new key I'd been given by the Realtor after he'd had the locks changed prior to my arrival, opened the door, and then stepped into the entry. The floor was damaged and would need to be replaced, and the wallpaper was peeling and would need to be stripped, but the rooms were totally empty, and empty rooms, I knew, even those in disrepair, were preferable to rooms filled with well-meaning friends who were unable to deal with your grief and wanted to help but felt helpless to do so.

The entrance to the home was large and airy and opened up to twin staircases spiraling toward the second story. I'd been told the house had three stories of living space, ten bedrooms, eight baths, and a large living area consisting of several rooms including a parlor and a library, on the first floor. I was also promised the property included a separate guesthouse that could be used as a mother-in-law unit. Apparently, the English gentleman who built the house back in 1895 had grand plans to marry his one true love and fill those ten bedrooms with chubby-cheeked children, but his dream, like mine, had never come to fruition, and so like me, he'd moved away. I knew there had been several owners between

Chamberlain Westminster and Bodine Devine, the man from whom I'd bought the house from. I wasn't certain of the entire history, but I supposed it didn't really matter.

While my move to the small town of Holiday Bay might not have been well-thought-out, the challenge to gently nudge the old girl back to her former glory had come at the perfect time. The house, I decided, would occupy my energy and my mind. Rehabilitating it would give me focus and provide a safe harbor from which I could fight my demons and finally begin to heal.

My long brown hair blew across my face as the front door blew open behind me. I whirled around, prepared to defend my territory, but all I found was empty space. I put a hand to my chest as my heart pounded. There was no one there; it was just the wind. I had to admit this huge, empty house had me on edge. It was almost as if I was half-expecting someone or something to jump out at me from around every corner. I took a deep breath, crossed the room, and reached for the door, preparing to remedy the situation, when a huge orange cat that had to be half mountain lion given its enormous size, darted between my legs and into the entry. "Shoo," I said as I waved my arms toward it. The cat looked at me with eyes as green as my own, took a few steps, turned, then trotted up the stairs. "Hey," I called after the feline. "You don't live here. You really can't stay." The cat reached the landing at the top of the first flight of stairs, turned to glare at me once again, and then continued down the hallway.

"Damn cat," I muttered under my breath. Life, I decided, was a cruel jokester. As if I didn't have enough to deal with, I now seemed to have a stowaway. Suffice it to say, Abby Sullivan was not now, nor had she ever been, a cat person, or any kind of animal person for that matter. I considered going after the cat but decided that perhaps it would find its way out on its own.

Returning my attention to the house, I walked into what, I assumed, was the main living area. The room was empty, but the hand-carved mantel, which framed the old stone fireplace, truly was a work of art. I ran my hand over the intricately carved surface and imagined the craftsman who had taken the time to get every detail just right. Hand carvings like this were rare these days, and I knew in my heart that the mantel, at least, would need to be preserved.

I turned back toward the room and considered the intricately carved crown molding along the ceiling. There were sections that would need to be replaced, but I supposed the damaged sections could be replicated. It would be a shame to tear down the original material if there was any way it could be saved.

I knew I'd taken on a project when I bought the place, but until I'd arrived and had a chance to look around, I'd had no idea how truly large a project it would be. There were a lot of rooms in need of attention, and so far it looked as if each room was the size of my entire condo back in San Francisco.

No need to panic, I assured myself, as I walked into the room I assumed had been previously used as a formal dining area. The house was going to be a lot of work, but I was up for the task. I'd just need to get organized, consider the entire project, and come up with a plan. From my experience, almost any project was possible as long as I broke it down into small steps I could handle so I wouldn't be overwhelmed by the magnitude of the work in its entirety.

I walked through the dining area to the back of the house, where I imagined I'd find the kitchen. The room was charming in an old-fashioned way. It was a large room with a lot of potential, although the appliances were ancient, the wallpaper peeling, and the cabinets dated. I supposed a total gut job would be required for this particular room, which meant that a hotplate and microwave might be good items to purchase, along with cleaning supplies, mousetraps, and maybe something that would provide the mountain lion, who I was certain was still prowling around upstairs, motivation to leave. What I needed, I realized, was a list. I took out my phone and opened an app. Taking action, any action, seemed like a move in a positive direction, which provided my slightly overwhelmed psyche with the illusion of control.

"Number one," I said aloud, "go to the store and buy food to last several days, and maybe an ice chest to store the food until the status of the refrigerator can be determined."

I walked over to the refrigerator and opened the door. I grimaced at the mess I found and then took a step back. Determining status didn't seem to be the issue so much as replacing the old unit with something less disgusting.

"Number two," I continued, as I walked around the room, opening and closing cupboards, "find a place to set up a home base while renovations are underway." I had brought an air mattress, sleeping bag, pillow, and jug of water with me, so once I'd figure out where to set up, I'd bring it all in and build a little nest. I had a stack of books, several bottles of wine, music on my phone, and even a propane light that would come in handy until I could deal with the electricity.

"Number three," I said into my phone, "have gas, water, and electricity turned on." I paused and looked around at the shabby interior. It really had been a while since the house had been lived in. "Number four," I added, "find a plumber and an electrician to check everything out before using the gas, water, and electricity."

There was a door leading off the kitchen that I assumed led to the basement that had been part of the listing. I turned the handle and opened the door to find wooden stairs descending into a dark space. Closing the door, I decided to leave a tour of the basement for another time and continued toward the rear of the house. The laundry area was large, but the windows had been boarded up, and the place was nothing more than a tangle of cobwebs. Taking a deep breath, I continued to the back door, which led out onto a huge deck that actually appeared to be in good repair. Climbing down from the deck, I headed in the direction of an adorable little cottage the Realtor had referred to as the guesthouse. From its location on the edge of the sea, I bet the view from this little place would probably be even more spectacular than the one from the house. Climbing the steps to the wraparound porch, I took out the second set of keys I'd been given and opened the door. I wasn't expecting much, given the state of disrepair of the main house, so when I opened the door and stepped inside, I was more than pleasantly surprised. The cozy space was dusty, but it looked as if it had been recently renovated and appeared move-in ready. I smiled as I noticed the large stone fireplace on one wall of the main living area. I could imagine how cozy it would be to curl up in front of the fire during a winter storm. The fireplace had a gas insert that looked as if it had been recently installed, but I supposed I should have it checked it before I used it. I picked up my phone and added *fireplace guy* to my list.

The living room, which featured hardwood floors and pale gray walls, opened up to a small but newly updated kitchen, which, thankfully, appeared to have working appliances. The space was charming and modern, with granite countertops and updated cabinets. I knew the cottage had two bedrooms, one in the front that looked out over the now-overgrown garden, and one at the back, overlooking the sea.

I poked my head into one of the two bathrooms. The dark gray granite countertops, like those in the kitchen, looked new, which thrilled me, but the cabinets, while updated, had been painted a dark green. Not really my color, but I could always repaint, and the room looked as if it would be adequate once I had the water turned on. Things were definitely looking up, I decided as I headed to the larger of the two bedrooms. The room had a door at the rear that I assumed opened out to a private deck.

"Wow," I said as I took in the view. It was simply amazing.

The dark gray of the winter bay in the distance was bordered by a lush green forest currently covered with a layer of snow producing an absolutely stunning contrast. The entire shoreline looked to be uninhabited, with the exception of a single dwelling in the distance, perched on the edge of the sea. A feeling of peace rose as the serenity of the landscape wrapped itself around me like a warm hug. I'd always found the sea to have a calming effect on my nerves, even during the worst of times.

Here, I decided, as I took in a deep breath of fresh sea air, was where I'd build my nest. Here in this little guesthouse, where I could both wake up and fall asleep to this spectacular view. I'd need a bed, and possibly a dresser, but for now I'd blow up my air mattress and set it next to the huge glass doors, which I planned to wash as soon as I got my supplies. It would be from this perfect spot, in this little house, that I'd read, dream, refurbish, and heal. I knew the journey to making the main house habitable would be a long one. I knew the road to healing would be even longer. But for the first time since I'd packed my SUV and merged onto Hwy 80 east, I actually believed both might be possible.

Heading back to my SUV, I grabbed my laptop and travel bag. I went back to the cottage, making the first of many trips. Once I had the vehicle unloaded, I sat down at the kitchen counter on one of the stools left behind. I took out my laptop and opened my mail app. I used my phone to take a photo of the fantastic view, then attached it to an email.

I started at the blank page for several minutes as I worked up the courage to continue. I had done a lot of difficult things in the past year, but for some reason, writing this email seemed harder than most.

Dear Annie,

Greetings from Maine. I've attached a photo of the view from the little cottage where I plan to begin rebuilding my life. Isn't it fabulous? I know you're concerned that I've descended into madness and am no longer in control of my mental facilities, and I understand your trepidation at the choices I've made since the accident, but I needed to do this despite your fears. It would mean so much if you could find it in your heart to understand and support my choice.

Love,
Abby

I read the email through, then let my finger linger over the Send button. Part of me wondered why I bothered, but another part realized that making things right with the only family I had left was a necessary step if I really wanted to rebuild my life.

Recipes

Triple Cranberry Sauce – submitted by Nancy Farris

Sweet Potato Casserole – submitted by Patty Liu

Minestrone Soup – submitted by Sharon Guagliardo

Pumpkin Cookies – submitted by Pam Curran

Triple Cranberry Sauce

Submitted by Nancy Farris

1 cup frozen cranberry juice cocktail concentrate, thawed
⅓ cup sugar
1 12-oz. pkg. fresh or frozen cranberries, rinsed and drained
½ cup dried cranberries (about 2 oz.)
3 tbs. orange marmalade
2 tbs. fresh orange juice
2 tsp. minced orange peel
¼ tsp. ground allspice

In a small saucepan, combine the cranberry juice concentrate, sugar, fresh or frozen cranberries, and dried cranberries. Cook over medium heat until the berries pop, about 15 minutes.

Remove from the heat; stir in the orange marmalade, orange juice, orange peel, and allspice. Transfer to a small bowl; refrigerate until chilled.

Sweet Potato Casserole

Submitted by Patty Liu

3 cups cooked mashed sweet potatoes
½ cup orange juice
½ cup milk
1 tsp. vanilla
½ cup sugar
½ tsp. salt
3 tbs. butter or margarine, melted
Cinnamon to taste

Topping:
3 tbs. butter or margarine, melted
½ cup brown sugar
⅓ cup all-purpose flour
1 cup pecans, chopped

Preheat oven to 350 degrees. Spray a shallow
casserole dish. In a large mixing bowl, combine sweet
potatoes, orange juice, milk, vanilla, sugar, salt, 3 tbs.
melted butter, and cinnamon; beat until fluffy; pour
into casserole. For *topping,* combine 3 tbs. melted
butter, brown sugar, flour, and pecans in a med.
mixing bowl; sprinkle mixture over potatoes; bake 35
minutes or until topping is brown and potatoes hot.

Serves 8

Minestrone Soup

Submitted by Sharon Guagliardo

¼ cup olive oil and more for garnish
8 green onions, sliced, or 1 med. onion, chopped
2–3 med. carrots, peeled and chopped
3 stalks celery, chopped
Salt and black pepper to taste
3 large potatoes, peeled and cut into 1-in. chunks
2 cans chicken broth
3 cups water
2 cans stewed tomatoes, chopped
1–2 med. zucchini, peeled, cut into 1-in. pieces
1 bunch escarole, chopped
1 can Great Northern or cannellini beans, drained and rinsed
1 can kidney beans, drained and rinsed
Freshly grated Parmesan cheese
Salt and pepper
Garlic powder and oregano

In a large pot, heat ¼ cup oil over med. heat. Add onion, carrot, and celery. Sprinkle with salt and pepper to taste. Cook, stirring often, for 10–15 min. or until vegetables begin to soften and darken around the edges.

Add potatoes, sprinkle with salt and pepper. Cook, stirring occasionally, for 5–10 min., or until vegetables are nicely browned.

Add broth and water, stirring to scrape up any browned bits on the bottom of the pan. Add tomatoes and bring to a boil, and then lower heat to a simmer. Cook, stirring occasionally, for about 15 min.

Add zucchini and escarole, raising heat if necessary, to keep mixture at a steady bubble. Cook until vegetables are very tender, another 10–15 min. Stir in the beans and cook for 3–4 min. Add salt and pepper if needed. Add a little garlic powder and oregano to taste.

Top bowls with Parmesan cheese and a drizzle of olive oil.

Makes 6–8 servings

Pumpkin Cookies

Submitted by Pam Curran

1½ cups sugar
½ cup Crisco shortening
2 eggs
1 cup pumpkin
1¾ cups flour
½ tsp. baking powder
½ tsp. baking soda
½ tsp. cinnamon
½ tsp. salt
1 cup chopped pecans

Mix all ingredients well by hand. Place by tablespoons on a greased and floured cookie sheet in a 350-degree oven about 10–12 min. or until brown.

Books by Kathi Daley

Come for the murder, stay for the romance.

Zoe Donovan Cozy Mystery:

Halloween Hijinks
The Trouble With Turkeys
Christmas Crazy
Cupid's Curse
Big Bunny Bump-off
Beach Blanket Barbie
Maui Madness
Derby Divas
Haunted Hamlet
Turkeys, Tuxes, and Tabbies
Christmas Cozy
Alaskan Alliance
Matrimony Meltdown
Soul Surrender
Heavenly Honeymoon
Hopscotch Homicide
Ghostly Graveyard
Santa Sleuth
Shamrock Shenanigans
Kitten Kaboodle
Costume Catastrophe
Candy Cane Caper
Holiday Hangover
Easter Escapade
Camp Carter
Trick or Treason
Reindeer Roundup
Hippity Hoppity Homicide

Firework Fiasco
Henderson House
Holiday Hostage – *December 2018*

Zimmerman Academy The New Normal
Ashton Falls Cozy Cookbook

Tj Jensen Paradise Lake Mysteries by Henery Press:
Pumpkins in Paradise
Snowmen in Paradise
Bikinis in Paradise
Christmas in Paradise
Puppies in Paradise
Halloween in Paradise
Treasure in Paradise
Fireworks in Paradise
Beaches in Paradise
Thanksgiving in Paradise – *Fall 2019*

Whales and Tails Cozy Mystery:
Romeow and Juliet
The Mad Catter
Grimm's Furry Tail
Much Ado About Felines
Legend of Tabby Hollow
Cat of Christmas Past
A Tale of Two Tabbies
The Great Catsby
Count Catula
The Cat of Christmas Present
A Winter's Tail
The Taming of the Tabby

Frankencat
The Cat of Christmas Future
Farewell to Felines
A Whisker in Time
The Catsgiving Feast

Writers' Retreat Mystery:
First Case
Second Look
Third Strike
Fourth Victim
Fifth Night
Sixth Cabin
Seventh Chapter

Rescue Alaska Paranormal Mystery:
Finding Justice
Finding Answers
Finding Courage
Finding Christmas – *December 2018*

A Tess and Tilly Mystery:
The Christmas Letter
The Valentine Mystery
The Mother's Day Mishap
The Halloween House
The Thanksgiving Trip

Haunting by the Sea:
Homecoming by the Sea
Secrets by the Sea
Missing by the Sea
Christmas by the Sea – *December 2018*

The Inn at Holiday Bay:
Boxes in the Basement – *November 2018*

Sand and Sea Hawaiian Mystery:
Murder at Dolphin Bay
Murder at Sunrise Beach
Murder at the Witching Hour
Murder at Christmas
Murder at Turtle Cove
Murder at Water's Edge
Murder at Midnight

Seacliff High Mystery:
The Secret
The Curse
The Relic
The Conspiracy
The Grudge
The Shadow
The Haunting

Road to Christmas Romance:
Road to Christmas Past

USA Today best-selling author Kathi Daley lives in beautiful Lake Tahoe with her husband Ken. When she isn't writing, she likes spending time hiking the miles of desolate trails surrounding her home. She has authored more than seventy-five books in eight series, including Zoe Donovan Cozy Mysteries, Whales and Tails Island Mysteries, Sand and Sea Hawaiian Mysteries, Tj Jensen Paradise Lake Series, Writers' Retreat Southern Seashore Mysteries, Rescue Alaska Paranormal Mysteries, and Seacliff High Teen Mysteries. Find out more about her books at www.kathidaley.com

Stay up-to-date:

Newsletter, *The Daley Weekly* http://eepurl.com/NRPDf
Webpage – www.kathidaley.com
Facebook at Kathi Daley Books –
www.facebook.com/kathidaleybooks
Kathi Daley Books Group Page –
https://www.facebook.com/groups/569578823146850/
E-mail – kathidaley@kathidaley.com
Twitter at Kathi Daley@kathidaley –
https://twitter.com/kathidaley
Amazon Author Page –
https://www.amazon.com/author/kathidaley
BookBub – https://www.bookbub.com/authors/kathi-daley

FEB 1 9 2019

Made in the USA
San Bernardino, CA
02 November 2018